BLACK ENTRY

- a novel -

by

Regis P. Sheehan

First Edition Design Publishing
Sarasota, Florida USA

Black Entry
Copyright ©2021 Regis P. Sheehan

ISBN 978-1506-907-43-7 PBK
ISBN 978-1506-906-29-4 EBK

December 2021

Published and Distributed by
First Edition Design Publishing, Inc.
P.O. Box 17646, Sarasota, FL 34276-3217
www.firsteditiondesignpublishing.com

ALL RIGHTS RESERVED. No part of this book publication may be reproduced, stored in a retrieval system, or transmitted in any form or by any means — electronic, mechanical, photocopy, recording, or any other — except brief quotation in reviews, without the prior permission of the author or publisher.

The opinions and characterizations in this book are those of the author, and do not necessarily represent official positions of the United States Government.

Dedicated to the memory of
Captain Bernard G. Albertson

-US Army-

Graduate of Duquesne University Army ROTC
Pittsburgh, Pennsylvania

Killed in Action
April 17, 1971
Age 24
Long Hai Hills
Phouc Tuy Province
Republic of South Vietnam

Captain Albertson met his death by hostile action while attempting to load a wounded South Vietnamese soldier onto a hovering medical evacuation helicopter

Requiescat in Pace

"... He that spies is the one that kills ..."

Irish Proverb

Other Novels/Novellas by the Author

SUPPLICANT
The prelude to the 9/11 attacks of 2001 -

SICARIO
The hunt for Pablo Escobar in Colombia -

SURROGATE
Narco-Terrorism in the Caribbean -

SUCCUBUS
A North Korean diplomat attempts to defect to the West -

www.Sheehan-Fiction.com

Contents

Author's Note i
Glossary of Acronyms ii

Prologue - Project Tiger 1
One – Kolya 3
Two - Jayhawk 8
Three - Hadrian 13
Four – Sarpi 16
Five – Schutzwall 22
Six - Sepes 28
Seven - Carriage House 33
Eight - Reflections 37
Nine - Resolute 41
Ten – Tuyet 44
Eleven – Cos 49
Twelve - Prospect 52
Thirteen - Tate 54
Fourteen – News From The North 57
Fifteen - Long Tieng 59
Sixteen – Hopper 65
Seventeen - Minerva 69
Eighteen - Wandering Souls 72
Nineteen – Crown Colony 79
Twenty – Despedida 81
Twenty-One – Encounter At Ap Bac 84
Twenty-Two - Sotu 88
Twenty-Three – Special Action 90
Twenty-Four – Unrest 96
Twenty-Five – Station Hospital 98
Twenty-Six – Vann 100
Twenty-Seven – Jason 102
Twenty-Eight – Sacred Sword 104
Twenty-Nine - Lyre 110
Thirty – The Monk 111
Thirty-One – Dragon Lady 114
Thirty-Two – Gone Astray 115
Thirty-Three – Sog 117
Thirty-Four – Easy 118
Thirty-Five – Xa Loi 119
Thirty-Six - Ambo 120

Thirty-Seven – Go Cong...122
Thirty-Eight – Fact Finding..124
Thirty-Nine – Big Minh...125
Forty – Jocko 127
Forty-One – Coup 128
Forty-Two - Summit 131
Forty-Three - Plain Of Reeds...134
Forty-Four – De Silva...137
Forty-Five – 34-Alpha..139
Forty-Six - Exodus...141
Forty-Seven – Tonkin...144
Forty-Eight - Monumento..146

Acknowledgements...152

Author's Note

This is a fictionalized account of *PROJECT TIGER*, the Central Intelligence Agency's clandestine efforts to penetrate North Vietnam with indigenous (largely South Vietnamese) agent teams in the early 1960's.

This project encompassed some 36 operations into the North over a period of three years.

While many of the descriptions of CIA agent teams and activities that follow are historically accurate, others are wholly fictional.

All of the historical CIA operations have been long since declassified and are available to the public.

GLOSSARY OF ACRONYMS

APC-Armored Personnel Carrier
ARVN-Army of the Republic of Vietnam (South Vietnam)
ASA-US Army Security Agency
BOB-Berlin Operating Base (CIA, West Berlin)
C-123-High wing, two-engine, propeller-driven transport Aircraft
CI-Counterintelligence
CIA-Central Intelligence Agency
CIDG-Civilian Irregular Defense Groups (South Vietnamese)
COS-Chief of Station
DC-4-Low-wing, four-engine, propeller-driven transport aircraft
DCOS-Deputy Chief of Station
DMZ-Demilitarized Zone
DDP-Deputy Director for Plans (CIA)
FE-Far East Division (CIA)
FMLN-Communist insurgents (El Salvador)
GDR-German Democratic Republic (East Germany)
GVN-Government of the Republic of Vietnam (South Vietnam)
LDNN-South Vietnamese SEALs
MACV-Military Assistance Command – Vietnam
MfS-Ministry for State Security (East Germany)
NLF-National Liberation Front (VC)
NCO-Noncommissioned Officer
NSAM-National Security Action Memorandum
NVA-North Vietnamese Army
NVOB-North Vietnam Operational Base (CIA)
OSS-Office of Strategic Service
PASF-Peoples Armed Security Forces (North Vietnam)
PDJ-Plain of Jars
RVNAF-Republic of Vietnam Air Force (South Vietnam)
SEAL-US Navy commandos (Sea Air Land)
SF-Special Forces (US Army Green Berets)
SEPES-South Vietnamese intelligence agency
SOE-Special Operations Executive (British – WW2)
SIS/MI6-British intelligence service
SSPL-Sacred Sword of the Patriots' League (CIA project)
SOG-Studies and Observations Group
SOTU-State of the Union Address

STOL-Short Takeoff and Landing (aircraft)
T-10-Standard US military parachute
USG-US Government
VC-Viet Cong
VIAT-Vietnamese Air Transport Company

PROLOGUE - PROJECT TIGER

"*Saigon CIA Chief of Station William Colby directed the initial covert operations into the North - designated Project Tiger - from 1961 to 1963 ...*

"*Eventually Colby would characterize Tiger as only a 'modest effort' with the goal of establishing resistance guerrilla operations. To the personnel involved it was something more than 'modest' ...*

"*Colby had personally acknowledged being 'well aware that black entry operations against the Soviet Union and Eastern Europe to be unfruitful' ...*

"*Still, in spite of those views, Colby neither suspended nor cancelled any of the ongoing black entry or maritime sabotage missions and continued to send in as many teams as could be trained.*"

Hancock and Wexler
"Shadow Warfare: The History of America's Undeclared Wars"

ONE - KOLYA

Oberweisenfeld Army Airfield
Munich, West Germany
March 15, 1954

The faintly luminous glow of his wristwatch read 2320 hours. Nearly midnight.

As expected, and planned for, the Operations Building was largely deserted by that time of night. The solitary figure on the ground floor of the structure shook his head, stuffing his hands into the pockets of his overcoat. With little else to do, he continued to gaze hopefully out of the window at the empty airfield.

The man loitering at the window was known to the Americans at the airfield and the locals alike only as *Kolya*. Although he was just easing into middle age, Kolya had already developed a shambling, careless appearance – both in dress and demeanor. He evidenced a set of sloping shoulders that supported a somewhat jowly face and a set of pale blue eyes that were chronically bleary in appearance.

Nevertheless, a casual dismissive assessment of the man would overlook an incisive mind and an absolutely driven personality. Hardly a dashing figure, by no means did he fit the popular image of a secret intelligence officer.

At the moment, Kolya focused his attention on the broad pane of glass before him. He appeared to be engrossed in the errant pathways described by droplets of rain as they splattered against the surface, beaded onto the glass, and gradually streaked away.

Beyond the glass was a cloudy expanse of dark German sky. Not so many years ago it would have been threatened by the approach of Allied bombers. Times have changed. The threat had now been pushed further eastward.

He was aware of a distant growl of thunder echoing troublingly in the distance. By his estimation, the storm seemed to be moving away from his location.

Kolya doffed his overcoat and continued to wait. He could use another drink.

Given the intensity of his concentration, one might think that someone's life depended upon what he was seeing. That was, in fact, the case. Four people's lives would be more accurate. Or eight lives, if you were to include those of the aircrew – which the latter most surely did.

The doors of the building creaked as a gust of damp wind hit them. A struggling radiator in the corner of the entryway hissed angrily in response. Up until that point, it had mainly served to boost the aroma of burnt coffee in the bleak enclosure.

Kolya sincerely hoped that the normally pessimistic meteorological guys were right this time around. Despite the dark clouds looming overhead and a band of light rain in a fifty-mile radius of the airfield, they advised that the storm was clearing up nicely along the proposed flight path.

Yet, the operational decision as to launch or not to launch had been his alone. That was the least of his problems. Given the Weather Ops advisory, he defaulted to his pre-scripted plan. Without a doubt, the mission officially was a go.

The planned route of travel would carry his charges out into the skies over eastern Germany, through Austrian and Czechoslovak airspace, and finally into the territory over the Ukraine. The majority of the flight would uncomfortably involve transit of what were termed *denied* spaces.

The mode of conveyance for this particular flight would be an unmarked multiengine transport of British manufacture. A battered veteran of the waning years of World War II, it had been specially configured for the delivery of personnel and supplies by parachute.

Kolya fought the urge to glance yet again at his wristwatch. No need to give in to his nervous habit. He was aware of the time. Painfully well aware.

Slightly over an hour ago, he had been ensconced at the opposite end of the airfield, sitting alone at a small conference table. The scarred table was in an anonymous, secluded building that served as the mission staging area. The tabletop itself was bare, but for a chilled bottle of Russian vodka and five pristine, cut crystal glasses.

Kolya had been waiting patiently for the men who would be traveling that night. Well into the second year of his tour in Munich, he was no stranger to the drama that was largely of his own making.

His study of the light reflecting in the facets of the stemmed glassware had been interrupted by the rumble of a vehicle as it pulled up to the door. The vehicle squeaked to a halt and killed its engine. Straightening up, he could hear doors opening and closing, followed by the subdued voices of a number of men in the anteroom.

Finally, the inner door opened, and four familiar figures trooped into the conference room. Each garbed in single-piece outfits, drab olive green in color, that were quite accurately called *jumpsuits*. Their demeanor betrayed a mixture of anticipation and nervousness.

Kolya knew each of them in-depth. All were single, whether thru divorce, death, choice or happenstance. They were all volunteers who had been carefully selected and then thoroughly trained. Moreover, they were also fairly well paid by local standards.

He was intimately acquainted with the men, having been in frequent contact with them on a near daily basis over the last several months.

But the one who he knew best was the diminutive man standing in front of him. That was Vasyl, the thirty-four-year-old team leader.

As was the case with the other men, Vasyl was what had previously been known as a *displaced* person.

A native of the Ukraine who had been gathered up to serve in the German Wehrmacht as an infantryman, Vasyl had been part of the drive toward Leningrad in 1941.

Fortunately, in his case, he was wounded on the way to northern Russia and was medically evacuated, thereby avoiding the frozen tragedy that ensued for his comrades. Later, caught up in the post-war chaos, Vasyl fled to the west and eventually found himself living in a refugee camp in the American Zone of Germany.

Like the others this evening, Vasyl's face was drawn, pale and tight. He was feeling the stress of the moment. And why not? If the conditions were right, within a few hours, all four of them would be exiting an aircraft in flight, with the goal of safely dropping into Communist-controlled territory to the east.

They were his agents, and Kolya was their case officer. As such, he was their manager, their mentor and the purveyor of their confidence, misplaced though it might occasionally be.

Although neither Vasyl nor any of his companions were privy to the classified details, they were part of an intensive CIA operation code-named AERODYNAMIC. The goal of the operation was the infiltration of native-born agents into the Ukraine to collect intelligence and foment dissatisfaction against the regime. AERODYNAMIC was itself but a subset of an overarching CIA project, termed RED SOX, which oversaw the penetration of the Soviet Union as a whole.

Following his pre-departure tradition for teams such as these, Kolya twisted the cap off of the vodka bottle and proceeded to charge each of the glasses with a generous pour. Acutely aware of the drama of the moment, he clinked the rim of his glass delicately against each of theirs and then held it at face level.

"To your success," he said. "*Zdorov'ya*."

"*Zdorov'ya*," they echoed. They paused momentarily. Without another word, all five of them tossed the vodka back in a single swallow and clapped the empty glasses back onto the tabletop.

Although the brief ceremony was clearly at an end, Vasyl held up a thin, tentative hand. "And we thank you Kolya," he said, fingering the empty glass, eyes visibly moist with tears. "We thank you for giving us this opportunity to contribute to the liberation of our country."

Kolya shook his head dismissively. It took no measure of acting to feel the emotion welling up within himself. "It is *our* honor," he said. "You are patriots. You are heroes. God be with you all."

All were silent as the four men left the building and re-boarded the blacked-out van that awaited them just outside. The van would transport them across the field to the plane. There, the jumpmaster would assist them into their parachutes and see that they were situated in the webbed bulkhead seats.

Kolya, in the meantime, climbed into his battered VW and cruised back over to the Operations Building. There was little more to be done on his end.

* * *

Kolya was still perched by the wide window when he heard the footsteps of an Army buck sergeant who noisily trotted down the stairwell from the control tower.

Kolya turned and looked at the NCO expectantly. "Yes?"

The ruddy-faced NCO gave him a double thumbs-up. "It's up and gone, sir," he reported. "Your bird just went wheels-up at 2352 hours."

"Thank you, Sergeant," Kolya said, latching onto his overcoat and hat. "I appreciate it."

He needed to drive back to his office. The office, which was located in downtown Munich at the Army's facility at McGraw Kaserne. There, he would fire off a short message to the Station Chief, based in Frankfurt, and that – for the moment - would be that.

TWO - JAYHAWK

Saigon
Republic of South Vietnam
June 5, 1962

The *Freedom Bird.*

That was the generic name given to the American commercial airline flights that carried US personnel out of South Vietnam and back to the relative safety of the United States.

Once back home, the public response to the veteran troops for their service in a foreign combat zone was not enthusiastically positive. Quite often, the reverse was the norm. The returning troops were frequently assailed with allegations of being war criminals, murderers, baby burners and worse.

The comparison of Vietnam vets with the earlier returnees of World War II or the Korean War could not have been more extreme.

There was no generally accepted term for those flights that transported young Americans *into* the Republic of South Vietnam, other than *Replacement Flights*.

One of the Replacement Flights into Saigon in the Spring of 1962 carried a lanky young man named Jay Laird. He was otherwise known to his cronies and colleagues as *Jayhawk*.

Dark-haired and square-jawed - some in college had teased him for his faint resemblance to classic Greek statuary - he was largely unimposing in most respects. Nevertheless, Laird was in fact a freshly minted Operations Officer of the Central Intelligence Agency. Not surprisingly, he was traveling into Vietnam under what was termed *official cover* - in his case, that of a Department of Defense civilian employee.

A native of the small eastern Kansas town of Gardner, Laird was a 1957 Poli Sci graduate of the University of Kansas. At KU he was more of a scholar than a jock. Although he had done well in high school basketball, his sports try-out in KU was a total bust. *High school hero to college zero* was the phrase he vividly recalled.

While he otherwise fully enjoyed the time he spent KU in Lawrence, Laird felt the urge to expand beyond the boundaries of the Midwest. He began to suspect that there had to be something more in life for him.

Following his graduation from KU, Laird spent an uneventful year or so in the environs of Kansas City, briefly seeking his fortune on the edges of the corporate world of finance. When that did not pan out, he headed east to American University in Washington DC. His new goal was a graduate degree in International Relations - and then see what came next.

Fate soon intervened unexpectedly, coming in the form of an uncle who spent World War II as a member of the Office of Strategic Services, or OSS. Pulling more than a few strings, Laird's sympathetic Uncle Joe secured an interview for his nephew with the organizational successor of the OSS - the CIA.

The initial session was followed by a lengthy series of follow-on interviews, examinations and an uncomfortably intrusive background investigation. At long last, however, the procedure culminated with a vague conditional offer of employment, which he accepted.

Months later, following his onboarding and orientation at the Langley headquarters, Laird was dispatched to his initial course of tradecraft training at *The Farm* in southeastern Virginia.

In due course, Laird graduated with respectable grades and evaluations. In rapid order, he was given a brief period of home leave, briefed on his upcoming assignment to Vietnam and wished the very best of luck. He was then given his tickets and sent on his way to his virgin tour at Saigon Station, Republic of Vietnam.

He was committed to the purpose. JFK was the President of the United States, and Laird was a more or less faithful Catholic and a Democrat. All was looking up for him.

* * *

As was the norm, the destination of the inbound flight was the Tan Son Nhut airbase. Although technically a South Vietnamese Air Force facility, initially opened by the French in the 1920s, Tan Son Nhut was largely operated and run by the US Air Force.

"Not quite so bad," Laird thought as he absorbed the weather outside of the protective metal shell of the aircraft. It felt humid. Temperatures were pushing the mid 90's, threatening an afternoon rain.

As he deplaned with the others, a minor distraction appeared that rattled the air overhead. Sheltering his eyes from the tropical sun, he caught sight of a green US Army helicopter as it clattered along above the far end of the Tan Son Nhut runway.

The helicopter was a Bell UH-1 variant - the *Huey* that was quickly becoming synonymous with the war in Vietnam. The barrel of an M-60 machine gun protruded from the Huey's open side door, its gunner scanning the territory below with casual menace.

Like a tourist, he craned his neck to follow the chopper's path until its drone faded and it soared out of sight to the west of the city.

Saigon, baby. The Pearl of the Orient. That's what he heard anyhow.

Welcome to the war.

* * *

Along with the other arriving passengers, Laird climbed aboard a dark blue Air Force shuttle bus that took them to the Personnel Reception Station at the other end of the field. As they rattled along to their destination, he could not help but notice that a mesh of metal caging covered the windows. Their purpose was to ward off thrown hand grenades or similar fiendish devices.

Upon arrival at the Reception Station, they filed off the bus and into the welcoming arms of the personnel system. As Laird shuffled along with the rest of his fellow passengers he was hailed by an unimposing man in civilian clothing.

"Jay Laird," the man said. He appeared to be an out-of-shape American in his mid-fifties. His statement was less a question than a declaration of fact.

"That's me."

"Jim Koval," the other said. "Welcome to Vietnam. I'm your new boss."

"Good to meet you," Laird said.

"Let's hope that remains the case," Koval said. His tone did not convey optimism. "You can skip the military reception procedures. Baggage claim is over here."

Having expected something just a bit grander for his initial entry into the war zone, he nonetheless trailed along behind the man as instructed. He noticed that his expedited arrival processing attracted a combination of envious and questioning glances from some of his fellow new arrivals.

After collecting his baggage, Laird again followed Koval out to the parking area and loaded everything into a battered white Toyota Land Cruiser. A Vietnamese driver maneuvered them through the military checkpoint and into the streets, which were choked with exhaust fumes and clogged with buses, motorized bikes, taxis and heavy military trucks. Another vehicle, presumably in a security role, followed them closely behind.

Within forty-five minutes, they pulled into a large secured compound on the northern edge of the city. A modest sign on the wall, in both Vietnamese and English, proclaimed the compound to be the home of the *Indochina Aid and Development Foundation*.

"This isn't the embassy," Laird commented, dismounting from the Land Cruiser.

"No, it is not," Koval agreed. "Good call. Let's go up to my office, and I'll explain."

Laird dutifully accompanied the older man through the doors of the main building and traipsed up two flights of stairs to his boss' office. Once seated, Koval pulled two chilled cans of beer from a small refrigerator. After puncturing the tops of each with a metal church-key opener, he passed one over to his new recruit, which the latter gratefully accepted.

Both of them took a moment to sit back and savor the first taste of the brew.

"As you accurately noted," Koval finally began. "This is most certainly *not* the US Embassy. This is the offsite headquarters of NVOB - what we call the North Vietnam Operating Base. It is also called *Project Tiger*.

"This is your new home for the next year or so," he added.

Laird did not try to hide his confusion. "Uh, well, with respect, I think there's been a mix-up of some kind here," he said. "I've been assigned to the Political Action Section in the Station. Not," he waved a hand absently "... whatever this is."

Koval nodded. "All well and good. That was true until the day before yesterday when Tate came down with a case of diverticulitis. He went out on an emergency medical evacuation. Not quite the heroic exit he was hoping for."

"Who's Tate?"

"The officer you are replacing."

Laird sat mutely, absorbing the sudden change of plans.

"This has been cleared by the COS," Koval said, referring to Bill Colby, the CIA Chief of Station. "We have a higher priority than Political Action. So, you're mine now. Snap in."

Laird sat silently for a moment, drinking his beer. "And what is it that we do here?" he asked.

"I'll tell you what we *don't* do here," Koval began. "We don't deal in government corruption, coup plotters, crooked colonels, mad monks or even enemy order of battle... Our remit is the main target. North Vietnam. More to the point, dispatching agent teams north and using them to gather information. That and nothing else."

Laird shook his head. "I have no training or experience in that."

"You will have," Koval assured him. "Soon."

THREE - HADRIAN

Vicinity of Hai Phong, North Vietnam
June 5, 1962

An unarmed, multi-engine aircraft pierced the night sky over North Vietnam that very same night. Officially, it was chartered to a commercial firm that billed itself as the *Vietnamese Air Transport Company* or VIAT. The true ownership of the company was quite otherwise.

The crew members of the airplane were all contracted Chinese Nationalists. The human cargo of the flight was comprised of South Vietnamese agents who were employed and trained by the Central Intelligence Agency.

The passengers were members of a CIA team that was code-named HADRIAN. The team included three Vietnamese agents: the team leader Huyen, the radio operator Lac and the scout Tien. All were weighted down with their operational gear and outfitted in olive green jumpsuits and plastic goggles for eye protection. On top of all of that, for each, was a canvas pack holding a blackened T-10 nylon parachute.

As the moment of decision approached, none were entirely confident of the dangerous mission awaiting them.

The objective of the team was the South China Sea harbor at Hai Phong. The area was located some fifty-five miles east of the North Vietnamese capitol of Hanoi. Enemy territory for certain. The CIA was highly interested in the activities and logistics of the harbor area - most especially the degree and type of Soviet shipping.

By June of 1962, fraternal Communist support for the Hanoi government was a well-established fact.

In January of 1960 an agreement was signed in Moscow assuring the Vietnamese of Soviet technical and economic assistance extending from 1961 to 1964. Likewise, in 1961 at the 16th session of the United Nations General Assembly (UNGA) in New York, the Soviet Union proposed that 1962 be the year of the total elimination of colonialism. Going further, Moscow demanded an end to the wars of foreign aggression and the dismantling of all foreign military bases.

China, for its part, was the first nation to establish diplomatic relations with North Vietnam. In December of 1961 it sent a military mission to Hanoi, pledging its support to Hanoi against American *aggression and intervention.*

None of that was troubling the minds of the HADRIAN team as the plane neared the drop point. They were more concerned with the minutes, hours and days immediately ahead of them. While all three had been trained in parachuting - by both day and night - this was to be their first operational jump into what was termed as a denied area.

The VIAT jumpmaster appeared to be distracted. In reality, he was focused on a message coming through the intercom in his headset from the front of the plane.

Nodding, he looked up to the HADRIAN agents. He gave them two thumbs up and then broadly displayed five widely splayed fingers.

Five minutes to the drop point.

Huyen, the team leader, silently nodded his understanding. Following his lead, Lac and Tien did likewise.

Double-checking to ensure that he was affixed to his safety line, the jumpmaster stood and waddled back to the rear door. As he pulled the door open, the blast of the external wind began to roar, suddenly chilling the cabin temperature.

After peering outside, assuring himself of a clear exit, the jumpmaster straightened up and summoned the team forward.

Huyen came up first. He positioned himself nervously in the doorway as the jumpmaster checked his straps and verified the position of his chute.

Behind him came Lac. As the radio operator, he was carrying the heaviest baggage of the team. The radio, set in a satchel was affixed to his chest, counterbalanced the parachute on his back.

After his main chute opened, Lac would release the container holding the radio set, letting it dangle on a line below him - so as not to be separated from his equipment upon landing.

Tien, the scout, came up last and took up a position tightly behind Tien.

The goal, as practiced, was to get all of the men out of the aircraft as quickly as possible. This would hopefully preclude any wide dispersal of the team on the landing zone.

The jumpmaster held up two fingers and shook them for emphasis.

Two minutes out.

Huyen glanced at the ground rushing along below. It was total blackness, as far as he could tell. Huyen returned his gaze to the space in front of him. Less than 200 miles to the north was the border of China.

One minute out.

"Stand by! Stand by!" the jumpmaster shouted in English, a language they all shared - to one degree or another.

Suddenly the jumpmaster slapped Huyen on his shoulder. "Go! Go! Go!" he yelled.

Whispering a silent prayer to his gods, Huyen stepped through the open door of the aircraft and into the hands of the inevitable.

As Huyen disappeared, Lac stumbled forward under the weight of his gear and followed him into the nothingness.

Tien moved to the door and grasped the frame, as he had been trained. When he showed a bit of momentary hesitation, the jumpmaster helpfully shoved him out of the door, sending him tumbling into the atmosphere after his teammates.

The jumpmaster pulled the door closed and secured it.

The drop completed, the VIAT crew made for a course that would take them back to South Vietnam.

FOUR - SARPI

NVOB - Saigon
June 6, 1962

Laird groggily awoke late the next morning. It was his first morning in Vietnam and his first experience with the unpleasant reality of jet lag.

After cleaning up and dressing, he made his way down the stairs and outside into the open air. His destination was the admin building that also contained the dining facility. All about him the compound quietly buzzed with a sense of purposeful, understated activity.

As Koval had advised him, the quality of the food in the dining hall was substantially above that which he could have expected at a US military base. Not that he had any basis for comparison. And it was all free.

Uncharacteristically hungry, Laird was on his second helping of American-style bacon and eggs when a man approached his table and sat down across from him. He was a thin, pale-faced, figure with longish black hair.

"Laird?... Jay Laird? Also known as *Jayhawk*?" the other said, extending a hand.

A pair of round, wire-rimmed eyeglasses offset his mustachioed, gaunt face. At least initially, he appeared to be a better fit for a rock concert attendee, rather than whatever this place was.

"That would be me," Laird answered, tentatively shaking the stranger's hand. "And you are?"

"Paul Sarpi," the other said. "Your new best friend."

"As in how?"

"Since you've been recently diverted to us here at NVOB from Main Station, I've been designated as your sponsor. Nice to meet you."

"A last-minute replacement, I'm told," Laird said, masking a shred of resentment. "Thanks to nothing more than a case of diverticulitis."

"Right you are," Sarpi agreed. "You're filling in for John Tate. Solid guy. Former Green Beanie. He was flown out of here with a busted colon. Should be back in the States by now."

"Sounds painful," Laird observed, taking another gulp of coffee.

"Not the glorious tour finale he would have wanted for himself," Sarpi said. "But, knowing John, he might be back someday. Or not... Finish up with that grub, and I'll read you in on the program. If you're up to it."

"Hitting the ground running, are we?" Laird mused.

"More like sprinting," his sponsor grinned.

* * *

"So, welcome to Project Tiger," Sarpi said once they were seated in the muted confines of his shielded and sound-proofed office. He pulled a sheaf of classified folders from his safe and spread them out across the desktop. "Or, more formally, the North Vietnam Operational Base.

"As Jim Koval probably already told you, here at NVOB we are all about North Vietnam and nothing else. Developing indigenous agent teams and inserting them above the DMZ for operational purposes," Sarpi said.

"I see," Laird said vaguely.

"As our newest Case Officer, you will be inheriting some of the ongoing teams that Tate was running. And you will also be responsible for gearing up new ones. Obviously."

"And that's what you do, as well?" Laird asked.

Sarpi leaned back in his chair and chuckled softly. "Me? Uh, no. No offense, but I don't fool around in the minutia of other people's lives."

"You don't? So, you do - what?"

"I'm just the modest Base Reports Officer here," he said, although his tone indicated anything but that. "That's my job. You Case Officers are the fighter pilots. I restrict myself to observing events and reporting the same back to Headquarters. Hopefully, keeping everybody straight on the facts as a result. That much and no more."

"Clean hands, clean heart," Laird observed flatly.

"You got it," Sarpi replied. "I sleep well... Pretty well anyhow."

"Sarpi," Laird speculated, moving onto a new, safer subject. "Italian then?"

"Better than that," Sarpi said. "*Venetian*. Named after my distant ancestor - Fra Paolo Sarpi of *La Serenissima*, the Most Serene Republic of Venice."

"Never heard of him."

"Who has?" Sarpi conceded. "He was a Catholic monk of the Servite religious order in Venice back in the late 1500s. He pushed for a Venetian church, separate from Rome. That led to a papal interdict of the whole of Venice. In fact, there's a statue of him right there in Venice, if you ever get there. It's next to the place where he was attacked and nearly killed by papal assassins..."

"Papal assassins?"

"Dagger through the head," Sarpi said. "Does that count? Lived through it, in any event."

"So, a rebel more or less."

"No doubt of that," Sarpi agreed. "There's contrarian genes in my make-up. I wonder how I ever made it into the Agency in the first place."

"Good point," Laird admitted.

"Yeah," Sarpi said, turning to the folders. "So much for ancient Italian history. Here's what's happening in the here and now. Specifically, involving you."

He unrolled a topographical map of North Vietnam onto a side table. "This great undertaking of ours kicked off right about... uh, here," he said, indicating a point on the North Vietnamese-Laotian border. "Son La Province. That is where a team code-named CASTOR parachuted in. Happened last May 1961. It was our first attempt to put people in there."

"What became of them?" Laird asked, orienting himself to the contours of the map.

"Radio silence," Sarpi replied dourly. "We now suspect that they were caught and killed pretty quickly."

"I see."

"Team CASTOR was followed by teams ECHO in June and DIDO in July. All dropped into the same general area. All quiet. All probably captured and killed. Sorry to say."

Laird studied the map carefully. "Who's doing the drops?" he asked. "Air Force?"

"Not very likely," Sarpi scoffed. "The drops are flown by our own VIAT crews."

"Which are?"

"Vietnamese Air Transport Company," Sarpi said. "A proprietary civilian airline owned by us and flown by Nationalist Chinese crews. Technically, a Delaware corporation. If you must know."

By which, he meant, a CIA shell company chartered in the state of Delaware. Even Laird knew that much.

"The North Vietnamese security services are that good?" Laird asked, pondering the green and brown contours lines of the map.

"Sadly, they are," Sarpi said. "And our allies in the South Vietnamese services are highly permeable, to say the best of them.

"On the other hand," Sarpi continued, "as of the beginning of this year, Headquarters views the operation as largely being successful. Teams are still there, and reports are still coming in."

"But you don't agree," Laird prompted.

"I am not the Director of Central Intelligence," Sarpi replied.

"Anything active now up north?"

"Glad you asked," Sarpi replied, returning is attention to the map sheet. "In February of this year we dropped a *Montagnard* team called EUROPA into Hao Binh, just outside of Hanoi. Still active.

"Then, in April, we dropped a six-man team of Thais, called REMUS, into Laos. They crossed into the Dien Bien Phu area and may still be in good shape. That is what we hope and expect, in any event."

"Looking better," Laird said.

"Well, not so fast," Sarpi cautioned. "Just this past May we lost three more teams - EROS, ATLAS and TOURBILLON. All dropped in. All pretty much gone, as far as we can tell."

Laird pushed back into his chair and breathed a sigh of exasperation. "This sounds like a pretty damned expensive undertaking in terms of human life," he said.

Sarpi shrugged noncommittally. "Not so new in our business though."

"Meaning?"

Sarpi put the end of a ballpoint pen into his mouth. "They ever mention an old operation called VALUABLE FIEND to your class back there at The Farm?"

Laird rolled his eyes upwards in thought. "Not that I recall," he said at last. "But it has an interesting name. I'll give it that."

"Pop quiz," Sarpi announced brightly. "Which country is the only Chinese Communist ally in Europe?"

"Okay, I know that one," Laird smiled. "Albania."

"You are correct, sir," Sarpi affirmed, waving the pen. "And that is where VALUABLE FIEND came into the picture."

"Okay, Fra Sarpi," Laird smiled. "Enlighten me."

Sarpi folded his legs to get a bit more comfortable. "This was soon after World War II. Around 1949. Early morning in the Cold War," he began. "Sorry. No Chinese at this point in the story though."

"Okay."

"It was the Agency's first effort at paramilitary operations in a denied area," Sarpi explained. "The Iron Curtain had enveloped Albania, and we wanted to take it back. As did the Brits. The idea didn't seem so unlikely at the time since Albania had fairly weak connections with Moscow. Compared to the rest of the Eastern Bloc countries at least.

"So, the Agency, in cooperation with the British SIS - or MI6, if you prefer - began launching agent teams into the country both by air and by small boat landings over several years. The overall objective was to break Albania away from Soviet control and give the West an early win.

"Actually, FIEND was the name we gave to our bit of the project. VALUABLE was the moniker on the British end. Both with essentially the same goal."

"And?"

"And it generally went to shit," Sarpi admitted. "Most - if not all - of the agent teams were caught and imprisoned or killed by the Communist security services. FIEND was shut down about five years later. Sometime around 1954.

"Similar deal in Korea," Sarpi continued. "Early 'fifties. That one was called Operation AVIARY, this time using US Air Force crews to drop ethnic guerrilla teams into North Korea. About the same success rate."

Left unsaid were similar post-war black entry operations conducted in Poland, the Baltics and Manchuria. With comparable results.

"Great story," Laird observed. "Uplifting tale, considering the circumstances. Thanks."

"Suck it up, son. See any relevance to what we are doing here?" Sarpi probed.

"I guess we have a bit more experience now."

"We do," Sarpi said. "Later on, in the 1950s, the Agency was into something called AERODYNAMIC. The goal that time was to drop a series of agent teams - native Ukrainians and others - into the Ukraine to foment an uprising against the Soviets."

"And how'd that one go?" Laird asked.

"The Soviet Union is still there," Sarpi said.

"What does Koval think of that?"

"Think of it?" Sarpi repeated. "Back in the day, he was a Case Officer right in the thick of it. Ran the drops of multiple agent teams into the Ukraine himself."

Laird reflected on that momentarily. "You seem to know our boss pretty well."

"I should," Sarpi replied. "We did our last tour together before coming here. In Berlin."

FIVE - SCHUTZWALL

Berlin
August 17, 1961

The clandestine observation post was situated in a darkened corner apartment overlooking Friedrichstrasse. Ordinarily, the dinner crowd would fill the busy street below at that time of day. Now, however, their numbers were greatly accentuated by the onlookers who stood about in sullen groups to frown and gape at the unwelcome new developments in their midst.

"Eighteen-twenty hours," the younger one commented, glancing at his watch. He was a support officer of the Base, called into play that evening due to staff shortages. "Should be just about time."

"Yeah," the older one agreed. "Just about."

The older man - a seasoned forty-one-year-old veteran of the Korean War - braced his shoulder against the edge of the window and raised the binoculars to his eyes. Adjusting the focus, he carefully panned down the street to the crossing point.

"Bingo," he said. "Here they come."

As he watched, an olive green, four-door US Army sedan soundlessly pulled up to the crossing point and came to a full stop. The East German VoPo, or *Volkspolizei*, officer went to the driver's side of the car and peered inside.

The VoPo officer paused to take note of the vehicle's license number and markings. Then, with a curt inclination of his helmeted head, he pulled open the improvised gate. The driver of the sedan nodded in return and carefully navigated the sedan through the opening of the tangled obstructions, emerging into East Berlin – officially, the German Democratic Republic.

The older man at the OP grunted in satisfaction. "Okay, they're moving... And. They're across. Call it in to BOB."

The younger partner keyed the handheld mike. "This is Channel Three-Three testing this frequency at eighteen twenty-seven hours. How do you read me? Over."

The radio speaker hissed momentarily. "Roger. Channel Three-Three is nominal," came the thinly voiced response. "Good signal. Thanks for the call. Out."

"Out here."

The operator at BOB, or the Berlin Operating Base, would continue to send nonsensical radio checks to other locations for the remainder of the evening until dawn to mask their true activity, as they had been doing for the past week and a half. But for tonight, Three-Three was the only station that mattered.

* * *

Jim Koval, also known as Kolya earlier in his career, sat in the passenger seat of the olive-green US Army sedan. He unconsciously held his breath as they wove through the artificial interzonal barricade and exited onto the course of normal city streets once again.

That evening Koval wore the uniform of an American Army officer, bearing the gold oak leaves denoting the rank of a major. The driver, sitting next to him, wore the uniform of an Army staff sergeant. In reality, the driver, Miklos, was also an Operations Officer from the CIA's Berlin Base.

Neither, of course, were truly members of the military establishment. On the contrary, both were counting on the East German agreement to continue to respect the Four Powers' right of access to all parts of divided Berlin, regardless of the current tensions. This agreement was especially sensitive insofar as it pertained to the rights of the Allied military forces.

So far, so good, they thought. So far, so good.

The goal of the evening's excursion - aside from gleaning whatever collateral intelligence they could in terms of current conditions on the other side - was that of an emergency agent extraction. Their objective was a man whom the Base referred to as ASCOT.

ASCOT's true name was Egon Ralf Gerst. A man of modest appearance that belied a keen intellect, Gerst was a lieutenant colonel in the East German MfS or Ministry for State Security. Better known as the *Stasi*, the MfS functioned both as the internal secret police and the foreign intelligence arm of the Democratic Republic.

Trained as a foreign intelligence collector, Gerst was previously stationed in Finland. The tour had been his first assignment outside of the Eastern Bloc.

It was there, just outside of Helsinki, that he had clandestinely made contact with an official of the American Embassy. Once a face-to-face meeting had been arranged, Gerst wasted little time in offering his services to the West. He baldly admitted that his motivations included financial as well as political and humanitarian considerations.

Following the usual vetting procedure, involving a series of cables that bounced back and forth between Helsinki and Washington, his offer was accepted. Egon Gerst then became a registered and productive foreign agent of the Central Intelligence Agency. Unknown to him, his assigned code name was ASCOT.

Three years later, Gerst was back in East Berlin. This time he was assigned to MfS headquarters on Ruschestrasse. Even better, he was a staff aide to the powerful chief of the Stasi himself, the Minister for State Security Erich Mielke.

Upon arriving at the Berlin Base in 1960, Koval became ASCOT's case officer. Given the relative freedom of movement between the Soviet, British, French and American sectors, communication with the agent had never been all that troublesome. Nevertheless, the usual tradecraft precautions were followed strictly for Gerst's protection.

In recent months however, Gerst began to show signs of heightened stress levels. While such behavior would be normal and expected reactions for agents operating in hostile territory, Gerst was increasingly sliding above the norm.

Again and again, he reported that he felt himself to be under increasingly heavy scrutiny from his counterintelligence colleagues in the Stasi.

Koval, for his part, continued to assure Gerst that he was secure and that he was probably no more than a victim of his own fertile imagination. Above all, absent a true emergency, he wanted his agent to remain in place and continue reporting.

Parallel reporting from other sources in the GDR, or the German Democratic Republic, began to indicate the opposite, however. It was entirely possible that someone within the MfS hierarchy was beginning to look into Lieutenant Colonel Gerst a bit more closely than had been previously the case.

Reluctant to pull the plug on a well-placed source, Koval conferred with the Base Chief and his deputy. After a lengthy debate, the chief ordered that ASCOT should be withdrawn from his covert role as soon as practicable and given asylum in the United States.

The planned date for his departure was Saturday, August 12th.

What the Americans did not know was that August the 12th was also the birthday of Gerst's elderly mother, Emma. Gerst protested that the entire family normally celebrated the date. He countered that it would be preferable – and less alerting - to depart a day or two afterward.

Left unmentioned was the fact that Gerst felt he would be unlikely to ever see his mother again in this life once he fled to the West. He wanted to make the most of this final opportunity.

Bad timing on the agent's part, Koval reflected. Yet ASCOT was not to be deterred from his self-imposed schedule.

Things began to change significantly for the Berliners, East and West alike, late on the evening of the 12th. Events commenced fairly unobtrusively when the GDR security forces began their low-key call-up.

In the early morning hours of August 13th, at 0130 hours precisely, the well-concealed GDR plan swung into action. In one coordinated maneuver, the twenty-seven mile divide between East and West Berlin was suddenly and efficiently closed, trapping ASCOT inside. This was accomplished via the erection of a string of wooden sawhorses and coils of barbed wire barriers, all reinforced with armed personnel.

This was the beginning of what the East German state media would come to call the *Antifascistischer Schutzwall*, or the Anti-Fascist Protective Barrier. Westerners would refer to it more simply as the *Berlin Wall*.

As a result of the inauspicious timing, Koval and his partner were in the process of their circuitous route through the streets of East Berlin on the evening of the 17th.

While behaving as a routine Allied military fact-finding tour would, they were also watching for indicators of surveillance. They could not imagine a scenario in which they would not be followed while traveling in the Soviet Zone. Especially now.

Koval and Miklos continued their meandering car tour of the eastern side of the city, scrupulously avoiding any sites of military interest so as not to elicit any additional surveillance interest. Rather, they offered the profile of a simple showing-the-flag assertion of Allied rights of access. Such had been a common feature of life in all four sectors of the city, East and West.

For his part, Gerst had finished his day's work at his MfS office on the Ruschestrasse and walked out of the building as was his normal practice. He was ostensibly heading back to his apartment for the evening.

Gerst's work day had been routine in the extreme. The remainder of the evening decidedly would not.

He was well aware that one of the prime reasons for the erection of the barrier had been to stop the flow of East Germans to the West. That very day, in fact, workers had begun to bolster the crude wooden and barbed wire enclosures with the emplacement of heavy cinder blocks.

At the same time, streets leading into West Berlin were being permanently cut off. Contrary to the hopes of some officials in Washington and Bonn who contended that the obstruction was but a temporary ploy, the wall was solidifying and strengthening.

To his existing offenses of treason and espionage, Gerst was about to add yet another serious crime, that of *Republikflucht*, or Flight from the Republic. It was also a crime punishable by death, which could be administered to the offender on the spot by the VoPo border guards.

Choking down his nerves to maintain a calm exterior, Gerst headed directly to his regular U-Bahn station. Rather than going home to his wife, however, he was beginning the process that essentially mimicked the behavior of his American case officer.

He would spend the next hour or so trying to determine whether or not his fellow Stasi comrades were following him. If such was the case, he would put his planned escape on hold for a better time. If not, he would be leaving the GDR tonight. Forever.

* * *

Palming the steering wheel, Miklos simultaneously glanced at the luminous glow of his wristwatch. "Time," he said.

Koval nodded in agreement and peered into the rear-view mirror. "Looks clear to me," he said quietly.

"Same here."

"Then let's go up there and take a look-see," Koval concluded. "Go right in two blocks."

After a few more minutes, they saw the anticipated signal. It was mid-way down the dimly street. Hanging limply from a wooden pole was a tattered red and white workman's handkerchief.

Koval recognized it immediately. It indicated that ASCOT believed he was clear of coverage and ready for exfiltration.

Wordlessly, the Americans continued to drive along the nearly empty streets of East Berlin. Miklos was timing their approach to arrive at a specific deserted corner at precisely eighteen minutes after the hour.

They planned to execute an operational maneuver that the Agency referred to as *working in the gap*. In other words, they would take full advantage of the handful of seconds when they were fairly sure to be free of hostile surveillance. It was in that critically brief time gap that they would make their operational move.

"Here we are," Koval muttered tightly. There was no need to refer to the map sheet resting on his knee. "Go get him."

Rounding the corner, Miklos abruptly slowed the car while Koval reached back to throw open the right rear door.

At once, a dark figure dashed out of the shadows of a side alley. Without hesitation, the figure plunged headfirst into the rear seat. The rear door swung closed as they pulled away from the curb and accelerated back up to a normal traveling speed.

In the meantime, ASCOT had pulled open the back of the rear bench seat and rolled under it, wedging himself uncomfortably into the narrow compartment between the seatback and the trunk.

Koval jammed the seatback into position once again and turned his attention to the front. "Okay," he said. "Home."

With that, Miklos steered them back toward the border, again maintaining a sedate speed.

Twenty minutes later, they reached the floodlit official crossing point. After a perfunctory wave from the VoPo, they traversed the ramshackle border and entered West Berlin without incident.

ASCOT was no longer merely a spy. He was now a defector.

SIX - SEPES

Saigon, South Vietnam
July 20, 1962

Despite the straining efforts of the vehicle's air conditioning system, Laird was still sweating. Although armored for protection against small arms fire, the sedan was one of the older vehicles in the fleet and it was showing its age.

Laird was being transported - with what seemed to be painful slowness - through the congested traffic and mid-day heat of downtown Saigon. They were headed toward a meeting with officials of the host government. In view of the discomfort, he was thankful that he wasn't the one who was actually navigating the busy streets; that task was left to an ethnic Chinese NVOB staffer named Xiao Lin.

Better known to the American staff for his physical size and strength as *XL*, Xiao Lin was a combination of driver, bodyguard and aide de camp who had recently been assigned to Laird. A refugee from the North whose family had previously fought and died for the French, XL had been a trusted Agency asset for the past several years.

Laird was also accompanied on this cross-town trip by his boss, Base Chief Jim Koval. They were heading for Laird's first meeting with a South Vietnamese organization known as SEPES, which was the acronym of its original French title of *la Service pour les Etudes Politiques et Sociales*, or the Service for Political and Social Studies.

SEPES was, in fact, the intelligence section of South Vietnamese President Ngo Dinh Diem's *Can Lao* political party. It was a rich, if unofficial, source of Vietnamese agents for the CIA's clandestine operations. That was especially the case where the interests of NVOB were concerned.

As a new-comer to the post, Laird had spent the past several weeks reading files and getting acclimated to the operational environment of NVOB and its pace of activity. During that time, he was peripherally involved monitoring the activities of one of the indigenous teams North Vietnam - the one called HADRIAN.

On the night of Laird's arrival in Vietnam, the three intrepid South Vietnamese members of Team HADRIAN were parachuted deep into North Vietnam. Their destination was the port area of Hai Phong, on the coastal area just east of Hanoi. Their assigned mission was to observe and report on shipping activity in the port, with an eye toward future sabotage efforts.

Soon after the drop, the team leader radioed back to NVOB that they had landed safely and were proceeding to their objective area. Initially, the Base was elated at the news, as were the people at the Station. More importantly, so were the managers of the CIA's Far East Division back in Langley, then overseen by Des FitzGerald, himself a veteran of Far East, or FE, regional operations.

Three weeks after the insertion however, questions began to arise. The untroubled, rosy reports coming in from the HADRIAN team, welcomed though they were, ran somewhat contrary to the norm of the Project Tiger teams to date.

While Koval and the Station were happy with the HADRIAN results, Headquarters was beginning to express doubts. Paul Sarpi tended to agree with the growingly jaded assessment of Headquarters.

The fear was that - yet once again - the CIA team had been captured and compromised and was sending back false information, under hostile control. But this time, the information had appeared to be sound. It included facts that, if indeed provided by the North Vietnamese, would have been at least marginally damaging to them and their cause.

It was a conundrum that cried out for resolution.

The joint agreement between the parties was to send in yet another agent - this time a singleton - to report back on the success of HADRIAN. That singleton agent would be tagged as RESOLUTE. It would also be the first operation for Laird to manage.

* * *

At long last, the vehicle pulled up to the gate of a fairly isolated, fortified compound. After a preemptory check of their identity, they were admitted into the SEPES grounds. Leaving XL and the vehicle behind in the compound parking lot, Laird and Koval were escorted up to the fourth-floor offices of Vo Binh.

As Laird had been briefed, Vo was a trusted political operative. He was a grizzled, graying man of indeterminate age who was the primary SEPES liaison to the NVOB - and thus the liaison of President Diem himself.

An attractive, young Vietnamese woman greeted them in Vo's outer office and led them in to meet the man himself.

As they approached the desk, the older man rose to his feet and reached out to shake their hands. "I am Vo Binh," he announced somewhat unnecessarily. "And you must be Mister Jay."

"Just Jay", Laird replied. "Honored to meet you, sir."

Vo nodded happily and dropped back into his seat behind the solid wooden desk. "Mister Jay... Mister Jim," he mused aloud. "No Americans I work with seem to have any last names."

"We are an unimaginative people," Koval said, settling into his own chair. "Unlike your own."

"Don't judge yourself too harshly," Vo said, wagging a finger at him. "You have enough outside critics here for the moment."

Of course, Vo Binh was fully aware of their full names and professional associations. Both parties knew it. Polite cover, however, demanded otherwise.

As they settled themselves and exchanged in idle chit-chat, the young woman re-entered the office carrying a tray bearing glasses of iced tea and a plate of spring rolls.

"Cam on ban," Vo said, thanking her as she placed the tray on his desktop. Turning his attention to his guests, he added, "We will have lunch upstairs in the executive dining room once we have completed our business here today."

Laird and the young woman exchanged brief smiles as she dipped her head in a slight bow and quickly retreated from the room.

Vo leaned forward and raised his glass in a toast. *"Co vu,"* he said. Cheers.

"Co vu," the Americans replied.

"To business then," Koval said, setting his glass aside. "As you know, the last agent team that went North seems to have landed successfully and is reporting conditions in the port area. As assigned."

"I have seen those reports," Vo agreed.

"But," Koval continued, "there are those here at our office and in Washington who feel that they may have been captured and are being played back against us."

Black Entry

"Yet, you must admit," Vo said. "Our record of success against the Northern Communists has not been an, uhm, total success."

"You are being kind," Koval said delicately. "We have had many failures in the North. They are a capable enemy."

"But an enemy nonetheless," Vo added, unsmiling now.

"Clearly," Koval said. "Which is why we are here to confirm the next joint operation."

"Which you are calling... What?"

"RESOLUTE."

Vo frowned. "I am sorry. The meaning of this word escapes me."

"Brave," Laird supplied. "Fearless. Determined... It's kind of a British term."

"Ah. Oh, oh, I see," Vo replied. "I see. Good choice of words, then. And the duty?"

Koval readjusted himself in the confines of the stiff wooden chair. "The agent's job would be to parachute into the North and conduct surveillance on specific enemy activities," he said.

Left unsaid to Vo was the detail that the insertion point would be in the Hai Phong area. Once there, RESOLUTE's task would be to confirm or deny the reliability of the HADRIAN team.

Vo nodded, pulling a classified folder from the top draw of his desk. "The man we have in mind for the next mission should be suitable to your needs," he said.

"Yes?"

"Yes," Vo said, peering at the contents of the file. "He is a veteran ARVN soldier," he said, referring to the Army of the Republic of Vietnam. "He is a sergeant and a decorated combat veteran. A trained paratrooper as well.

"His family is from the South - Darlac Province. They are considered to be politically reliable. He is a volunteer for clandestine missions and fully understands the risks."

"The name?" Koval asked, producing a small notebook.

"Dao Duc," Vo said. "A good man. As I have said."

"Dao Duc," Koval repeated, jotting in his notebook. "Very good... If you are happy with him, then so are we. Jay here will be managing the RESOLUTE operation."

"Much success with Sergeant Dao, Mister Jay," Vo smiled, closing his folder.

"To us both," Laird said.

Vo passed the folder containing Dao's biographic details to Koval. Despite the favorable track record with SEPES, the Agency would run its own background checks on the prospective agent before considering him to be fully vetted for operational use.

The strictly business portion of the meeting concluded, the three men went up to the SEPES executive dining room, where they were joined by several of Vo's senior officers.

Nearly two hours later, after what was a heavily alcohol-infused luncheon of fine food and many toasts to the success of their joint efforts, they were escorted back down to the parking lot.

"Who was that girl in Vo's office?" Laird asked, feeling a bit of a buzz as they ambled over to the waiting vehicle.

"Girl?" Koval echoed, a bit fuzzy himself at that point. "Oh, her... Tuyet is her name. Been with Vo's office for the past year. She's a war widow. Husband was a pilot in their Air Force. Diem supporter. Obviously."

"Trustworthy?"

"About as much as any of them."

"War widow," Laird reflected. "And so, single."

Koval paused as XL caught the door of their vehicle for him. "You just got here, son, he cautioned. "Don't fall in love too fast."

"Yes, sir."

SEVEN - CARRIAGE HOUSE

Hoc Mon District
Saigon, South Vietnam
August 6, 1962

The Hoc Mon district is in the northeast section of Saigon. Still further to the northeast lay the Cu Chi area, later to be known for its extensive maze of Vietcong tunnels snaking into the city.

It was a Monday morning, and Laird again found himself in a vehicle with XL en route to a meeting place. The destination this time, within the Hoc Mon area, was known to the NVOB folks as *Carriage House*. At the time, it also contained the clandestine preparation site for a number of the agents destined for operations in North Vietnam.

Laird was passing the time by perusing a second-hand copy of the *Stars and Stripes* newspaper. Passing through the thin pages of the journal, he reflected that the more he worked in the intell field, the more he came to see its similarities with the world of journalistic newsgathering. The question being which was the more current and accurate.

Thumbing through the journal, he saw that it had been a newsworthy weekend. Back home, the Los Angeles police had found the body of Marilyn Monroe in her Brentwood house. A drug-induced suicide was suspected. The article rekindled rumors swirling about her relations with the President. Laird knew nothing about that, but he found the death of one of his adolescent sex idols to be troubling, to say the least.

On the international front, a leader of the anti-apartheid regime, the African National Congress in South Africa, had been arrested on charges of terrorism. His name was Nelson Mandela. South African authorities were claiming that he was both a Communist and a terrorist. The Mandela name only registered in a passing fashion with Laird.

Arriving earlier than planned, Laird and XL killed time in the small snack bar of the facility. Straddling chairs at a high-top table, they dallied over cups of heavily sweetened French coffee and a pair of fried egg sandwiches with thickly crusted white bread.

While he had some issues with the foreign policymakers of France, Laird reflected, he had no problems with their food choices. So far.

Finally, a stocky Hispanic man known to all as Fabian came to find them. Sporting a shaved head and a graying stubble of a beard, Fabian was an Agency contractor who ran the Carriage House training base. Texas-born, he was a Korean War veteran of Mexican parentage. As rumor had it, he was involved with the abortive Bay of Pigs operation – code-named *PLUTO* - just the year before.

The word at NVOB was that Fabian's involvement was in the Guatemala phase, preparing the recruits of *La Brigada* for the Cuban invasion. While the disaster that followed in PLUTO could hardly have been attributed to his actions, Agency wags debated whether his follow-on Saigon assignment was a promotion or a punishment for his efforts.

"You are Jayhawk, no?" he asked, shaking Laird's hand vigorously.

"I am, sir," Laird replied. "Glad to meet you at last. I've heard a lot about you."

"I can only imagine," Fabian said, acknowledging XL with a slap on the bodyguard's shoulder. "So then, let's go meet our man of the hour."

Leaving XL in the cafeteria, Fabian led Laird through a series of doorways and hallways until they reached a small conference room on the far end of the building. There, sitting at a long table alongside another Vietnamese employee, was the agent known as RESOLUTE. He was otherwise known as Sergeant Dao Duc, a combat veteran late of the ARVN's 5th Airborne Battalion.

Spotting the Westerner that he correctly presumed to be his CIA case officer, Dao leapt to his feet and bowed his head respectfully. He shook one of Laird's hands with both of his and muttered something in Vietnamese.

"He says that he is honored to meet you Mister Jay," the other man, the interpreter, said.

Drawing on his limited Vietnamese language skills, Laird replied in kind, "I appreciate your service and look forward to working with you."

Superficial formalities dutifully exchanged, Laird withdrew the classified RESOLUTE case file from his locked courier satchel and opened it on the tabletop. With the help of Fabian and the interpreter, he dug deeper into Dao's background.

Given his military experience, there was clearly little need for additional parachute training. Nevertheless, the VIAT aircrews would need him to do at least two low-level night drops into a heavily forested area for confirmation of his skills.

Much greater focus was paid to his technical familiarization with his communications equipment. Dao needed to be comfortable not only with the operation of the radio set but also with its upkeep and minor repairs. Likewise, he was to be schooled on the codes to be used and planned communications schedules.

Not the least of his training would deal with the geography of the Hai Phong area, which he had obviously never visited, and with the mission of the HADRIAN team.

Laird's agent was thirty-two years old, although he looked a bit older than that. He was born in 1930 in a small fishing village on the coast of the South China Sea. His birthplace was near the town of La Gi, which was almost directly east of Saigon.

The youngest son of a family of peasant fishermen, Dao had two brothers and three sisters. The parents, Laird noted, were now living in La Gi with their married daughters. His two brothers however, had been killed in the war. They fought for the Saigon government for reasons of their own.

Following the example of his brothers, Dao joined the ARVN as an enlisted soldier. After gaining a few years of experience, he volunteered for one of the parachute battalions and there excelled as a small unit leader.

Marrying late in life, by Vietnamese standards, Dao wedded a simple girl from a village near his ancestral home. Laird grimaced as he came upon that portion of his biography.

Dao's wife had been an unsophisticated country girl - Linh by name. She was seven months pregnant with their first child when a reinforced team of Viet Cong guerrillas entered her village. At the time, Dao was on operations elsewhere in the south.

The VC remained in the village all night and through the next day, conducting what they called *agitprop*, or agitation and propaganda exercises. When they learned that young Linh was not only the wife of an ARVN paratrooper, but was also carrying his child, they denounced her and quickly found her to be guilty of crimes against the people.

By noon of the following day, the VC hauled her, screaming with fear, to a tree on the outskirts of the village. There, after securing her against the trunk with rope, they disemboweled her with a machete.

Needless to say, Linh died an agonizing death, the tiny form of her unborn son lying in the bloodied dirt under her clouding eyes.

She was an object lesson to the other villagers who might have considered siding with the government. Lessons learned, the VC agitprop team hoped.

Several months later, a distraught and bitter Dao Duc learned of the SEPES office in the capital. Going through his company officer, Dao contacted SEPES and offered his services. He would do whatever was required in terms of revenge.

Laird looked up from his file, genuinely touched by the personal history of his newly acquired agent. "My friend, he said, "I am very sorry for the loss of your wife and child."

Listening to the translation, Dao nodded but remained unexpressive. "*Sat Cong*," he said flatly. Kill the Communists.

"*Sat Cong*," Laird agreed. "We will do this together."

EIGHT - REFLECTIONS

August 17, 1961
West Berlin

The officers of the CIA's Berlin Operational Base, aka *"BOB"* were justifiably proud of themselves. Their Stasi agent Egon Gerst, or ASCOT, had been successfully spirited out of East Berlin.

Even sweeter, they accomplished the rescue mission within a week of the closing of the East-West border via the initiation of the Berlin Wall.

The original ops plan, as submitted by Koval to the Chief of Station, had been to immediately bundle Gerst aboard an awaiting US Air Force transport at Tempelhof. From there, he would be flown out to the increased safety of the American facilities at Rhein-Main Air Force Base outside of Frankfurt in West Germany. At Rhein-Main, he would be medically assessed, initially debriefed and then forwarded on to the United States for further processing.

As it happened, the aircraft appeared to have plans of its own. While on final approach to Tempelhof, the flight crew saw issues with oil pressure on two of their engines. After touching down successfully, they were decidedly not going back into the air again that night.

The decision was made to hold Gerst in Berlin overnight until a fresh aircraft could be provided the next morning. Still, as short-handed as they were earlier in the day, the Base determined that the primary officers concerned with the extraction would maintain control over their agent for the remainder of his stay in West Berlin.

That being the case, Koval moved his charge to a BOB safe house and spent the night in an initial debriefing session. With him were two other Base officers - Miklos, who had accompanied him into the Eastern sector, and Paul Sarpi, the first tour Reports Officer who had been monitoring their progress from the observation post.

Each of the three Americans had assumed their impromptu debriefing roles. Koval, the case officer, would handle the interaction with Gerst. Miklos would play the host, ensuring a flow of snacks and drinks - while simultaneously providing armed security for the team. And Sarpi would take notes and operate the tapes to record the session.

It was past midnight as they settled down with their drinks - beer for Gerst, coffee for the Americans. Koval started with the standard threat questions.

"So, here we are," Koval said, ostensibly relaxing in his chair.

"Here we are," Gerst agreed. His English, as well as his Russian, was nearly perfect. There was no need for a translator, although all three Americans spoke a passable level of German.

"You can be assured that this area is well secured," Koval said. "You will be safe until we can get you out to Frankfurt in the morning."

Gerst nodded agreeably. In his view, the worst was behind him now. But there was also the issue of his family on the other side of the zonal border.

Koval took a sip of his coffee and leaned forward in his chair. "Before we move on to more substantive matters, there are some questions that we are required to ask of you."

"I understand."

Sarpi jotted a few notes on his pad, as much to describe the atmospherics as to record the data. He glanced up as Koval cleared his throat and began to speak again.

"Are you aware, Egon, of any Soviet or GDR, or other Warsaw Pact, preparations to launch a military attack on West Berlin at any time in the near future?"

"No. I am not."

"Or of any other violent provocations planned against the Western powers on this side of the zonal divide?"

"Unless they plan some response for my defection when they learn of it," Gerst shrugged. "No."

"Are you aware of any Soviet or GDR plans to strike West Germany or any of the NATO countries?" Koval continued.

"No."

"Are you aware of any Soviet plans to conduct a strategic strike against the mainland of the United States?"

A smile curled about Gerst's lips as he reached for his beer mug. It was duly noted by Sarpi.

"I am, or should I say that I was," he corrected himself, "a mere lieutenant colonel of the Stasi... How much strategic information do you think they gave me?"

"Probably about as much as Washington gives to me," Koval agreed with a grin, raising his cup to toast his agent. "But the answer is...?"

"The answer, my friend, is *no*."

"Understood. Let's move on."

As Sarpi recorded the session, his mind turned to the initial training that he had received at *The Farm*. During the early stages, they spoke of the ancient Chinese writer Sun Tzu, or Master Sun, he of the ancient *Art of War* fame.

Sun Tzu was widely known for his military advice via such oft-repeated aphorisms as: *"The supreme art of war is to subdue the enemy without fighting"* or *"In the midst of chaos, there is also opportunity."* After more than two thousand years, his advice still held true.

The Agency instructors at The Farm pointed out that Master Sun appreciated the arts of espionage as well as conventional military strategy. In his writings, he had specifically delineated five classes of spies. Although, the instructors cautioned, he was clearly speaking of what we termed as native agents, as opposed to our own professional *case officers* or *spy runners*.

The first of Sun's agent category was what he called the *local* spy or those recruited from among the population of the enemy state. These were the unsophisticated, yet often valuable and invisible, class of informers.

The next was the *inward* spy. In Sun Tzu's terms, this was a spy who is a recruited official of the government of the enemy's state. He or she would be a trusted source of information regarding the decision-making process of the opposition.

Following in the order was the so-called *converted* spy. A double agent, in modern terms. One who had been sent against us and was somehow caught, or was seduced, into working for us while simultaneously keeping his day job.

And then was the *doomed* spy. These are agents whose only purpose is to spread false propaganda or disinformation to the enemy and are then abandoned to their fate. Not a good reputational practice for any modern intelligence service.

Finally, Master Sun wrote of the *surviving* spy. These are the lucky ones who literally survive their time behind the lines and live to be exfiltrated and extensively interviewed for further study and analysis.

As he continued to scribble in his notebook, Sarpi reflected that Gerst was not only a converted and inward spy but - luckily for him - a surviving one as well.

Sarpi paused in his note-taking to glance up briefly. ASCOT's puffy face was already glowing with his sense of relief.

May they all be as lucky, Sarpi wished.

NINE - RESOLUTE

NVOB - Saigon
August 24, 1962

It was a sleepy Wednesday morning. Despite the hour, the day was already hot and clinging with dense humidity, given that it was late August in Vietnam,

The first thing after breakfast, Laird found himself in an increasingly familiar locale - the office of the NVOB Reports Officer Paul Sarpi.

"Ah, Jayhawk," Sarpi muttered, looking up from his croissant and mug of tea. "Good morning. *Ban khoe khong?*" How are you?

"*Toi khoe, cam on,*" Laird replied, drawing upon his limited reserves of Vietnamese and dropping into a chair on the other side of Sarpi's battered desk. I'm fine, thanks."

He peered at a set of papers that seemed to have engrossed Sarpi. "What'a 'ya reading?"

"A report, naturally. It's a summary of the conference in Hawaii last month," Sarpi replied, referring to the strategy session that had hosted by SecDef McNamara in Honolulu. He shook his head skeptically.

"What of it?"

"Just the stuff that Harkins had the *cojones* to say."

"General Harkins?"

"The same," Sarpi said. "Paul D. Harkins. MACV commander... Told McNamara that there's no doubt that we are on the winning side of this thing... Predicted that the Viets only need another year to finish off the VC."

"Did McNamara agree?" Laird asked.

"Looks like Mac thought the Viets needed something more on the order of three years to do the job."

"And what do you think?"

Sarpi grinned crookedly. "I'm only paid to write reports. I leave the heavy thinking to the bosses at the Station."

"Sounds good to me," Laird said. "Division of labor."

"Anyhow," Sarpi said, pushing the papers aside. "How are things at Carriage House?"

"All of it looked fine to me," Laird said. "For what that's worth."

"Um hmm." Sarpi took a bite of the croissant. "You met Fabian there, I assume?"

"I did," Laird said.

"Observations?"

"Uh, he's a bit of a character."

"That's been noted before," Sarpi agreed.

"Kind of an old-timer, don't ya think?" Laird frowned. "Maybe a little past his prime."

Sarpi shook his head dismissively. "Don't know about that part. Fabian's a real hard ass. Old school Agency. Like they say - knows where the bodies are buried... And maybe put some there himself."

"A trigger-puller?" Laird offered.

Sarpi nodded. "Back in the day, yes."

"Okay. *Mea culpa*. Anyhow, Carriage House is also where I met a Vietnamese named Dao Duc. He's an ARVN soldier and our agent for the RESOLUTE operation."

Sarpi pulled a worn notebook from a desk drawer and opened it. "And so, his status now is what?" he asked, reaching for a pen.

"Operational," Laird replied. "He was dropped last night just west of the Hai Phong area. His instructions are to move into the port area and send back details on the HADRIAN team."

"You were there for the send-off?"

"Of course."

"And you being Dao's case officer and all," Sarpi observed. "He's your baby. The first one out of the box. It must be a pretty nerve-wracking experience for you."

"You could say that," Laird admitted. "Like you said, I was there to see him off... Kind of a creepy feeling. Me back here on the ground and him flying off to the North toward... Towards who knows what."

"Welcome to the NFL," Sarpi quipped, taking a sip of the cooling tea. "That's what we do around here. Ask Koval."

"Yeah." Laird unscrewed the cap of a water bottle and took a long pull. "Anyhow, he landed safely a few hours ago and is now progressing on foot toward his objective."

Dao's objective was the same as that of the HADRIAN team itself - the Hai Phong harbor.

Situated at the mouth of the *Cam River* - *the* Forbidden River - Hai Phong was North Vietnam's most important maritime city. Re-supply visits by Soviet freighters was a regular and welcomed activity at the port. The Russian attention also made the area a focal point of CIA interest as well.

Sarpi scratched a few lines into his notebook. "The HADRIAN team has been in place for a little more than two months now," he said. "Regularly sending back detailed reports on port activity. HADRIAN has big fans at the Station. And back at Headquarters as well."

"And here at NVOB?" Laird prodded.

Sarpi shrugged with a thin smile. "I'm a skeptic. So, who knows?"

Laird stared at the Reports Officer for a few long seconds. "That doesn't fill me with confidence as to the welfare of my agent up North."

"Again," Sarpi said, not looking up this time. "Welcome to the League."

TEN - TUYET

Saigon, South Vietnam
September 1, 1962

Since his initial visit to the SEPES offices in late July, Laird had been engineering the schedule to allow him to handle the majority of the liaison matters with Vo Binh and his South Vietnamese intelligence entity. As developing manipulator of human assets, however, the overriding purpose of his ostensible volunteerism was strictly personal. His aim was to get closer with Vo's attractive female assistant, Tuyet.

Laird had recently taken the step of escorting Tuyet to a midday lunch at a small place close to her office. During the casual lunch, he learned that she came from a well-placed Saigonese family. Her father had been a university professor with political connections who studied history and law in Paris in the early 1930s. He was now semi-retired and considering a run for political office with President Ngo Dinh Diem's *Can Lo* party.

Happily, there seemed to be an element of mutual attraction that prevailed throughout their first unofficial encounter. Ever the optimist, Laird suspected that the portents were favorable.

After loitering in Vo's outer office in his most recent visit, Laird paused to ask Tuyet if she might be free and interested in going out to dinner on Saturday. As it happened, she was.

The following evening, again accompanied by his trusted CIA driver/bodyguard Xiao Lin, Laird swung by Tuyet's gated suburban residence and collected her. Their destination was a restaurant in the famed Caravelle Hotel in downtown Saigon.

Laird had tentatively arranged with XL that they were to be dropped off at the hotel for dinner and then picked up the following morning. If all went according to hopes and plans, that was.

Along with its neighboring Continental Hotel, the Caravelle, a local establishment with French origins, was one of the most prized locales in Vietnam.

Home to both the embassies of Australia and New Zealand, the Caravelle also housed the bureaus of various international news services. As such, it was thought to be a fairly secure location for social gatherings of all kinds.

In recent years the Caravelle had added a political dimension to its mystique. A group of Vietnamese politicos who were ardently opposed to the rule of President Diem had taken to meeting in its environs. Referred to as the *Caravellists*, they were well known both to SEPES and the CIA station. They were monitored accordingly.

Laird paused in the lobby to admire his date. In her off-duty guise, Tuyet was even more alluring to him than before. Her unblemished face had a delicate bone structure that belied her 26 years. With long black hair and dark eyes, her trim athletic figure was enhanced with a traditional *ao dai* – a blue silken dress with a long, thigh-length slit featuring her right leg.

Together they rode the elevator up to the Caravelle's well-appointed ninth-floor rooftop restaurant known as the *Champs-Elysees*. Overlooking the Saigon River, it offered a commanding view of the outskirts of the capital city.

As usual, the busy restaurant was doing what Laird's father would call a land-office business. The *maitre d'* greeted them warmly and led them to their reserved table next to a window. Peering out, the twinkling lights of the city slowly faded away as the view extended into the hinterland.

Unsummoned, a dignified elderly waiter appeared by the table to take their drink order.

"Scotch. Macallan, if you have it," Laird said. He suspected that the stores of liquor were heavily pilfered, or at least bartered, from US military Class 6 supplies.

"Certainly," the waiter said. "And you, madam?"

"White wine," she said. "*Sancerre*."

"Of course," the waiter said, disappearing once again.

"Thank you for bringing me here tonight, Jay," Tuyet offered, glancing about the room. "It's been a while for me."

"You've been here before?"

Tuyet nodded. "Just once," she said. "With my husband Thao. We came to celebrate his graduation from flight school."

Laird was, of course, already aware of the details of Tuyet's late husband. "Tell me about him. About Thao," he prompted.

"He was a good man," she murmured. "Caring. Handsome. From a good family. He could have easily avoided the war but he wanted to do his part for our country – so he enrolled in the Air Force, the RVNAF. He wanted to become a pilot."

"An honorable decision," Laird observed. "You all must miss him."

"He was a patriot," she agreed, nodding her head to indicate the pending arrival of the drinks.

The elderly waiter deposited the glasses on the table. He left them with dinner menus and again departed discretely.

Laird touched the rim of his glass against hers with a light clink. "Cheers."

"*A votre santé*," Tuyet responded.

Laird opened a menu and glanced at it absently. "And after his graduation from flight school?"

She smiled with a whiff of sadness. "As he had hoped, Thao became a fighter pilot. He was assigned to the 2nd Fighter Squadron in Nha Trang. He flew the American airplane that you would call the Skyraider."

Laird was familiar with the Douglas A-1 Skyraider. It was a single-seat, prop-driven plane. While its provenance dated back to the end of World War II, it was still a powerful aircraft that packed a punch. Combining wing-mounted cannon fire and rockets, it was more than applicable to the current struggle.

Although it was not appropriate to the moment, Laird recalled the fact that two RVANF pilots, also flying Skyraiders, had bombed the Independence Palace - the official residence of President Diem - just in February of that year. As motivation, the pilots claimed their belief that Diem was more intent on staying in power than in fighting the Viet Cong insurgency.

One bomb was said to have impacted a room in which Diem was present but failed to explode. Diem cited divine protection for his deliverance that day.

Of the two pilots, one was captured and jailed; the other escaped to Cambodia.

"You lived at the air base in Nha Trang then?" He asked, coming back into the present.

"No," she said. "Thao insisted that I stay here in Saigon with my family. Safer, he said."

"And then you lost him."

"A little over a year ago," Tuyet said. "They told me that he was flying in support of ground troops in a battle near Buon Ma Thuot when VC gunfire hit his airplane. He died in the crash."

"Still," Laird offered "A hero."

"I think so."

As if in a poignant underscoring of her tale, a series of silent explosions bloomed on the northern horizon beyond the window. Flares of red, streaked with yellow, dotted the blackness. Despite their elegant surroundings, it was clear that government troops were still in contact with the enemy not so very far away.

"I'm sorry," Laird commiserated. After a sip of his Scotch, he continued in a lowered tone of voice. "It must have been difficult for you. But you found a career to sustain yourself... How did you come to get your position with SEPES?"

Tuyet smiled thinly. "It was thanks to Thao's father. He is a cousin of Mr. Vo. My former father-in-law made the arrangements for me to work for him at my current office..."

"Good."

"I am appreciative," she said. "The work is important."

"It is."

After the waiter returned to take their dinner orders, Laird sought to lighten the mood a bit. Casting about, he saw a familiar face at a table across the room. Familiar to the Station, at least.

"See that fellow over there?" he asked, motioning to a florid, dark-haired Westerner who was sitting with three other men. Wearing an untucked short-sleeved white shirt, he was entertaining his dinner companions with a humorous tale of some sort. From their looks and demeanor, his tablemates appeared to be American military officers in civilian attire.

"No," she said. "Who is he?"

"One of the more notable war correspondents," Laird said. "His name is Peter Arnett. He's a New Zealander. Working for the Associated Press."

"I've never heard of him."

"You probably will," Laird assured her. "He's an active up and comer among the foreign press here. He's the one who first broke the story of the coup in Laos."

"Kong Le," she said. "The paratrooper captain." She was well aware of the incident, even though the rebellious captain only held power in Vientiane for a scant four months before being overthrown himself.

"Yes."

"So, we are dining with the famous?" Tuyet smiled, lifting her wine glass.

"More or less."

"And you, Jay," she continued. "Where in America is your home?"

"Kansas," he said. "A small farming town in eastern Kansas called Gardner. I doubt that you have ever heard of it."

"Kansas." Tuyet brightened after a moment. "I have heard... The Oz ghost. Dorothy. The dog Toto."

"The Wizard of Oz," Laird admitted. "That's us."

"Your family were farmers?"

Laird shook his head. "No. My dad owned – still owns – a farming supply company there."

A loud crack of thunder suddenly quieted the dining room. Their momentary fears of a bombing or mortar attack evaporated as a heavy gust of rain splattered against the window.

"The weather is turning," Laird observed. "If it keeps up, we'll get soaked taking you home."

"What are you suggesting?" Tuyet asked softly.

Laird shrugged. "Just that it might be better to stay here for the night..."

Tuyet reached across the table and covered his hand with hers in acceptance.

ELEVEN - COS

CIA Station – Saigon
September 14, 1962

It was a suitably bleak Friday morning. Though often thought of as a loosely enforced *Federal Friday* back home, it lacked the relaxed equivalence in Vietnam.

NVOB Chief Jim Koval had sought a meeting with his boss at his office. The request granted, he was perched on a chair next to a secretary in the outer office of the CIA Chief of Station, or COS.

Within moments of the appointed time, the COS' office door swung open, and a familiar, thin, bespectacled figure greeted him with a smile. "Jim," he said. "Phone call ran a little late. Come on in."

"Yes, sir," Koval replied, heaving himself out of the chair.

Bill Colby nodded and beckoned for him to go into his office. Koval nodded smilingly to the executive secretary and followed him into the inner sanctum.

The benign, bookish appearance of the COS belied his actual history. Despite his outward lack of flair, Colby had, in fact, been a member of the legendary OSS *Jedburgh* teams that had jumped into occupied France during World War II. There, his mission primarily entailed sabotage and providing whatever material assistance the Allies could offer in support of the resistance fighters. An awardee of the Silver Star, the third highest medal for valor, Colby had also seen later OSS combat service in Norway before the war ended.

He had been in his current Saigon slot since 1959.

"Okay, Jim," Colby said, as he settled in behind his desk. They were in a secure area where they could speak freely. "What's on your mind?"

"The negative trends with the operations in the North," Koval said.

"Specifically?"

"Most recently, issues with both teams HADRIAN and RESOLUTE."

Colby pursed his lips. "You'll have to refresh my memory."

Koval crossed his legs and folded his hands in his lap. "HADRIAN," he began, "was a three-man team that dropped into the Hai Phong area back in August. They were tasked with monitoring the shipping at the port. Specifically, we were interested in the Soviet freighter traffic coming in to resupply the NVA with weaponry and other logistical support."

"Okay," Colby brightened. "I recall it now... A fairly successful effort. Headquarters even forwarded some of their reporting to the White House. Well received."

"Very successful," Koval agreed. "Some would think maybe even a little too rosy, given the environment they were operating in."

"You said *'were',*" Colby said. "As in...?"

Koval grimaced. "One way or another, I'm not so sure that they are still with us."

"Well, as I said, the analysts in Langley were pretty happy with the product," Colby continued. "The information on Russian shipping seemed to match with other intel coming in from the reports of the Soviet/East Europe Division."

"If I may," Koval said. "It was not just the folks in Headquarters... Your own analysts here at the Station were pretty full-on for the HADRIAN reporting."

"As I remember, the Hai Phong data was an uptick in the quality of the product from the North."

Koval nodded. "Or, conversely, they may have just been wetting themselves with glee after getting so much bad news out of the North."

"Which is why..." Colby began.

"Yes," Koval interrupted. "Which is why we decided to send a singleton agent in to find out whether HADRIAN was too good to be true."

"RESOLUTE," Colby supplied.

"Right. An ARVN sergeant named Dao Duc. A guy with a grudge against the VC and willing to take risks. The plan was for Dao to operate in the harbor area but to do so unbeknownst to the HADRIAN team. He was to try, as best he could, to verify their activities back to us in NVOB."

"And I'm aware that his reports on the first team were on the negative side."

"More than that." Koval leaned forward in his chair for emphasis. "Dao thought that the HADRIAN team was operating under enemy control."

"Went bad?"

"That or they were caught and turned," Koval said.

"According to Dao, none of their reporting times matched with their appearance on the ground. So, either they were sending back information under Communist control, or someone else was sending it for them. Plus, they were not sending back reports of harbor activity that Dao himself was seeing."

Colby regarded his NVOB chief for a few quiet moments. "Are you sure that you aren't just flashing back to your AERODYNAMIC days in the Ukraine?"

Koval pondered for a moment, reflecting upon his *Kolya* time launching agents out of Munich. "I can't deny it," he admitted. "We dropped a shitload of loyal and trusting agents in to the Soviet-controlled areas back then. Most of them went to their deaths. I'm afraid that we are doing it again. Here. Now."

Colby picked up a mechanical lead pencil and began to scrawl doodles on a pad in front of him. "The North Vietnamese have a highly efficient security system. No doubt." He looked up at Koval. "They are the very definition of a denied operational area. And just because they have such a set-up doesn't mean we should avoid it. Just the contrary, in fact."

"I'm not disagreeing with the concept," Koval said. "I'm just getting tired of losing trained people who have placed their trust in us. For what purpose?"

Colby doodled for a few more quiet moments. "You know," he said at last. "My time here is coming to a close. I'll be shortly heading back to a Headquarters assignment."

"To the Far East Division," Koval supplied.

"Yep," Colby agreed. "My replacement will be John Richardson. COS now in Manila. Good man."

"So I've heard."

"I'd like to leave him with the best program possible," Colby said. "To include our aggressive efforts to penetrate our targets in North Vietnam."

"I understand," Koval said.

"Good," Colby brightened. "Good talk."

TWELVE - PROSPECT

**Outskirts of Saigon
September 18, 1962**

On the evening of the 9th, Laird participated in the launch of yet another agent team into the North that was under his purview. This mission was code-named PROSPECT.

The PROSPECT mission consisted of three local agents - both were South Vietnamese nationals named Sawn, An and Rian. While it was yet another intelligence-gathering operation, this one had a more distinctly lethal intent than many of the others.

The PROSPECT target area was the North Vietnamese province of Cao Bang. Located in the northeastern quadrant of the country, it bordered the Guanxi province of what was thought of as *Red China*.

Although China and North Vietnam were both Communist nations, their mutual history was far from amicable. Ho Chi Minh, in one of his less lyrical quotes, was once reputed to have said *"I would rather smell French shit for five years than to eat Chinese shit for a thousand years."*

The Communist chief of Cao Bang Province was an experienced political partisan and hardened war veteran named Luong Hanh.

He was more informally called *Luong Cu*, or *Old Luong*. The name was a bit of a stretch as he was only in his mid-forties. Nevertheless, his gaunt physical appearance bespoke the hardship of his life experiences. He had a complicated personal history.

Born in the neighboring northern Vietnamese province of Lang Son in 1919, Luong began his life under the experience of French colonialism in Indochina. In 1940 however, the forces of Imperial Japan invaded the country, displacing French rule.

As a politically aware young man, Luong was viscerally opposed to the occupying forces of the Empire. After several months of simmering opposition, he decided to take action on his own.

Initially, his activities were limited to low-level sabotage efforts combined with the distribution of nationalist leaflets and other forms of propaganda. When the opportunity first presented itself, he voluntarily engaged with the American OSS in the organized resistance struggle against the Japanese.

Slightly more than three years later, Luong emerged from the strife as an experienced and blooded warrior. By mid-1945, the Japanese were withdrawing, and the French authorities were reestablishing their control of the county.

Late in 1946, he agreed to become a covert agent for the French intelligence service, then known as the SDECE. That was, what could retrospectively be considered, a serious error in political judgment. Luong had secretly renounced the nationalist cause in favor of the colonialists.

France, however, departed the country following their consequential 1954 defeat at Dien Bien Phu. Luong was silent for several years as he made his way into the victorious Viet Minh political system.

Then in the later 50's, he re-emerged to offer his services to the CIA. Given his history and his potential level of access, his offer was quickly snapped up.

Over the past 20 months or so, Luong had gone dark, as the saying went. His loss as a source was troubling enough to the Saigon station. Worse was an analytic product from Headquarters in Langley.

For the past several weeks the Station Chief had been agonizing over a finding from the Far East Division that Luong had possibly – more like probably – reverted to North Vietnamese control. Of greater significance, they posed the theory that he might have been responsible for the high rate of loss of agent teams that had been dropped into the North.

The preferred manner of resolution: kill him.

THIRTEEN - TATE

NVOB - Saigon
September 16, 1962

Paul Sarpi met Jay Laird upon his arrival at the offices of the *Indochina Aid and Development Foundation*, better known to them all as the North Vietnam Operational Base or NVOB, that Monday morning.

"You're late," Sarpi challenged.

"Overslept," Laird said.

"That Viet gal?" Sarpi countered with a slight smirk. "Never mind," he said, shaking his head without waiting for a response. "I have a surprise for you."

"What?"

"Not *what*. More like, *who*?"

"Who then?"

Sarpi smirked. "Come along. I'll introduce you."

Together they trudged up a couple of flights of creaky wooden stairs until they reached the third landing. Turning a corner, Sarpi tapped smartly on the doorframe.

"Yeah, what?" a gruff voice barked in response.

Laird peered into the previously empty office space. Cramped behind the desk was a thickly built Black American. From the looks of his graying hair and bushy mustache, he was at least in his mid-forties.

Perched on a shelf of the bookcase behind his head, in an apparent position of honor, was a frayed dark loden green beret; the distinctive headgear of the US Army Special Forces. The identifying flash, or unit crest, was bright gold and blue in color.

"John," Sarpi announced. "This is the lost soul who was Shanghaied out of the Station to replace you after you left us with a busted gut."

"Poor bastard," the other said, rising from behind his desk and extending a hand. "John Tate".

"Jay Laird..." he said, taking the hand. "Looks like you're back."

"Clearly," Tate agreed. "Have a seat."

"Well, at that," Sarpi, said, "I'll go back to work and let you fellows get acquainted with each other."

Black Entry

They grunted in agreement as the Reports Officer scampered back down the stairs to his office.

"Coffee?" Tate asked reaching for a pot on a nearby hotplate.

"Yeah, thanks." Laird paused while the older man sloshed some coffee into a mug and passed it over to him.

"Where you from, guy?" Tate asked, taking a tentative sip from the rim of his own mug.

"Kansas."

"Kansas," Tate repeated. "Humph. Never heard of it." He added a slight grin to soften the reply.

"And you," Laird countered. "Judging from that decoration on your shelf, I'm guessing that you have an SF background."

Tate glanced up at the beret reflexively.

"You got that right," he said. "Signed up with SF long ago. *Snake-eaters*. Most recently with the 77th Group in Laos. Just around the beginning of all this horseshit."

Laird reflected on his briefing papers. "I'm not familiar with the 77th."

"Probably not," Tate agreed. "The 77th is no longer on the Army rolls. It was reconstituted as the 7th Group in 1960... I was over in Laos in late '59 when it was still the 77th. Some of our work was in cooperation with the French military. Our particular Mobile Training Team was set up in a place called Pakse. Ever heard of it?"

"No. Not really."

"Hell. Who has? Southern part of the country. Scenic enough, I guess... Not that I'm looking for any retirement property in the area.

"Anyhow, we were tasked with training the Laotians in counterinsurgency operations. Or at least trying to kick the ass of the Royal Lao Army into some kind of fighting shape."

"How'd that work out?"

Tate sniffed with a scowl. "Take a look at the reports. Or the evening news."

"And this included Kong Le," Laird asked, his thoughts going back to the recent dinner conversation with Tuyet at the Caravelle. "The paratroop captain who ended up overthrowing the government?"

"Negatory," Tate said. "A bit after my time. Never met the little asshole myself."

"Too bad," Laird offered lightly. "He sounds like he might be your kind of guy."

Tate casually gave him a middle finger and took another sip of coffee.

"And so, this was the *White Star* mission," Laird offered. That much, at least, had been amply covered in his pre-deployment training at Headquarters.

"Nah," Tate said. "It was before that. Our particular goat rope was called *Project Hotfoot*. The commander was Colonel Bull Simons. Great guy. Going places..."

Lard shook his head.

"The operation became known as White Star around '61. I was already gone by then. After I punched out, the Agency offered me a contract as a Paramilitary Officer. And here I am."

"Some career," Laird said approvingly.

"Yeah," Tate said. "Twenty-four years in the US Army. Serving all over the place with barely a scratch, aside from a case of malaria and a broken leg on an early jump. And then here I am sitting in a safe office in Saigon. My insides break open, and I get an emergency med-evac... Go fucken figure."

"Go figure."

Tate pushed his mug away and leaned back in his chair. "So, I hear that you have already launched the PROSPECT team. Correct?"

"Correct," Laird said. "They landed safely and have been up there for about a week now. HOPPER will be the direct action team. They are in isolation right now."

"And HOPPER will be launched from Long Tieng, right?"

"That's the plan."

"Okay," Tate said. "Koval wants me to go along with you to see that team off."

Laird stirred in his seat a bit.

"Hold on now," Tate said, raising a cautioning hand. "I'm not taking over your operation... "Think of me more as just a friendly uncle coming along for the ride. A mentoring kind of deal."

"Okay Uncle John," Laird said after a pause. "Welcome aboard... For the ride."

FOURTEEN - NEWS FROM THE NORTH

Saigon, South Vietnam
October 5, 1962

Sarpi was alone in his office, working on a quarterly report of the NVOB missions sent North. What he was seeing was not a boost to his morale. The damage was, in fact, far worse than anything he saw in his Berlin posting. The higher-ups back in Langley were likely to enjoy it even less.

He pulled a handful of manila file folders from his safe. Each was dully stamped with their multiple classification warnings. The folders were labeled TOURBILLON, EROS, ECHO and CASTOR.

His attention first came to that of Team TOURBILLON.

TOURBILLON was a sabotage team. On May 17th, a DC-4 dropped them into North Vietnam, having spotted the flame pots that been placed on the ground to assist on their aim. Their target was near the Laotian border, directly west of Hanoi.

Unfortunately for the members of the team, the reception signal had already been compromised. The flame pots were set afire not by the expected friendlies but by members of the PASF, or the Peoples Armed Security Forces – a militia under the control of the North Vietnamese Ministry of the Interior.

Adverse wind conditions blew most of the team members off course from their intended landing spot and away from the clutches of the PASF.

One member who was not blown off course was the Assistant Team Leader. He came in directly on target when his parachute became caught up in the limbs of a tree. It was then when he spotted the PASF troops closing in on him. Despite dangling from the branches of the tree, he opened fire on the approaching PASF. They returned fire during the engagement, killing him.

The remaining members of the team landed a bit further abroad and briefly escaped. Within two days, however they were captured, as well.

The North Vietnamese skillfully exploited the team's radio operator as a form of deception, with the goal of luring in yet more teams.

Saigon had dutifully accepted the TOURBILLON transmissions as authentic and, on May 27th, dispatched Team CASTOR.

CASTOR was on the ground for two days until they made contact with Saigon. Two days after that, they were captured. The team surrendered without a fight and went under North Vietnamese control.

On May 20th, the EROS team was parachuted into Thanh Hoa province just east of the Laotian border. EROS was a five-man team. Despite a successful landing, on June 20th, they signaled that they feared that they may have been compromised and were being closely tracked by the North Vietnamese.

Panicked and running out of food and other supplies, EROS was on the move. By August 5th they were again spotted and chased. As of the 29th of September, the PASF had killed one of the them and captured two.

The remaining two escaped into the arms of Laotian hunters. The Laotians then betrayed them to the North Vietnamese security forces.

On June 2nd Team ECHO was dropped at a location to the southeast of the known CASTOR team. A period of three weeks of silence followed their landing. When they did finally make contact, Saigon was suspicious of their communications. It seemed that their radio operator had been using an improper call sign. NVOB later learned that ECHO had been evading the PASF and running for the Laotian border when they were captured.

Sarpi could only hope that the future would bring better results for the teams.

FIFTEEN - LONG TIENG

The Plain of Jars – Laos
October 10, 1962

A military flight picked up the two men on the outskirts of Saigon just before dawn. After touching down in Vientiane, the somnambulant capital of Laos, they switched aircraft and continued to their destination via the auspices of the Agency's own contractor, *Air America*.

The familiar aircraft used for the shorter leg was a short takeoff and landing (or STOL) U-10 Helio Courier. The U-10 was a high-wing, propeller-driven Agency workhorse. Their destination was located in the Plain of Jars, also known in French as the *PDJ*, or *Plaine des Jarres*.

Laird and Tate were sitting side by side behind the pilot in the U-10, each with a side window view. All three were wearing headsets and mikes to enable them to communicate over the drone of the engine.

After a half-hour or so of uneventful flight time, Tate tapped lightly on the window with his knuckle to draw the other's attention. "There you are," he announced. "Right down there, son. Soak it in. Laos. The *Land of a Million Elephants*."

"Don't see any elephants," Laird mused, looking at the flatlands of Laos down below. "Lots of hidey holes for guerillas, maybe."

"Same-same," Tate replied, absorbing in the view. "For a place no bigger than Utah, it sure does manufacture enough shit for high drama, though."

Laird made a show of concentrating on his handwritten notes to mask his nervousness. The significance of what they were planning to do weighed heavily upon his Mid-West conscience, despite the strictures of his earlier training.

The PROSPECT team had been operating safely in the North for several weeks now. They had successfully accomplished their mission in that they had pinpointed the location of Province Chief Luong and had established his daily pattern of life. They signaled back to NVOB that all was ready for the entry of HOPPER: the kill team.

Glancing outside once again, Laird took note of the stark gray rock towers that began to sharply gouge up out of the earth, seemingly on their own initiative.

"Those things look almost prehistoric," he mused.

"*Karst* outcroppings, they call them," Tate answered.

"Karst?"

"Yeah. Limestone rock formations," he said. "They're all over the damn place up hereabouts. Apparently also found in China and Mexico and such."

"Eerie looking," Laird commented. "Spooky landscape."

"That's the least of it."

They lapsed into their private reflections as the Helio-Courier cruised along for another twenty minutes. The ridges of the highlands grew more pronounced the further north they traveled.

The temporary stillness of Laird's headphones was interrupted by the Spanish accented voice of the pilot. "Now coming up on the PDJ, gentlemen", he announced flatly. "Inbound. Twenty minutes out."

Scrolling along beneath their wings, seen and unseen, were the scattered sites of prehistoric, five-foot-tall man-made urns that gave the region its name. They were presumed to be iron-aged burial jars. As to the culture that emplaced them, nobody really knew for sure.

Looming up ahead of them, tucked into the valley between the hilltops, was a scarred green and brown conglomeration of tin shacks and muddy streets, reflecting the end of the annual rainy season. The single strip runway that sat at the end of the gritty township dominated the view.

The elevation of the strip was approximately 3,100 feet above sea level – about 1,000 feet higher than back in Saigon.

"Now on final," the pilot announced after several more, long minutes. "Gentlemen, that up there is LS Twenty-Alfa. Dead ahead... Strap in tight."

Laird shot Tate a questioned glance.

"Lima Site, Twenty-Alternate," Tate translated for the newbie. "Long Tieng International, for all intents and purposes."

The pilot guided the U-10 toward the single runway with practiced precision. It was, for him, routine. A combat milk run.

Coming in over the ragged threshold of the strip, the pilot cut power on the Helio Courier's single Lycoming engine. He eased back pressure on the yoke and held it until the wheels touched down, smoothly chirping along the roughly paved surface.

"And we're down," he commented, as if to himself.

As they taxied in, Tate pointed out a row of what appeared to be a series of silvery WW-II era, prop-driven fighter planes parked along the edge of the flight line.

"Those over there," he said. "Those are AT-28's. Fairly ancient dual seaters, yeah. Old US Navy trainers. But they can be some mean shit when armed with .50 caliber machine guns and rocket pods. The 28's might look like something from yesterday," he continued, "but they are real bastards in a ground support mission with our little pals at the stick."

Tate nodded to himself, recollecting some past battlefield memory. "If you doubt me, check with the Pathet Lao Commies up in the hills out there."

"I don't doubt you," Laird replied, taking in the view of the warbirds from another time.

Finally rolling to a stop, the Air America pilot locked the brakes and cracked open the side door. "And here we are," he announced a bit grandly. "Long Tieng. This is your stop, folks."

As Tate and Laird exited the U-10, pulling their backpacks along, a muddy and battered former US Army Jeep pulled up alongside to meet them.

"Welcome, Mister John!" the Jeep driver called. He was a wizened indigenous figure of indeterminable age. "Happy to see you here at Twenty-Alternate again. You have come!" he declared.

"Old Foom," Tate grinned, dropping his pack and stepping out to embrace the driver with genuine affection. "Again, I have come. So glad to see you, my old friend".

"And you too, Mister John... You are well?"

"As well as an old man can be," Tate said. "So far, the spirits are with me."

"And with me," Foom agreed. "It is all good."

Cognizant of Laird clambering down beside him, Tate added. "And this is my friend Jay. From Saigon. A good man."

"Mister Jay," Foom smiled, extending his gnarled hand.

"Foom," Laird smiled, taking the proffered hand with both of his.

"Where's Tony?" Tate asked, chucking his pack and Laird's into the Jeep.

"Not here," Foom said. "Mister Tony is out of camp. Working. Back tomorrow. Says see you then."

"And General Pao?" he asked.

Vang Pao was the leader of the CIA-funded Hmong army headquartered at Long Tieng. An experienced natural warrior, he fought alongside the French against the Japanese during the Second World War and later against the forces of the Communist Viet Minh.

"The General is with Mister Tony now," Foom said. "Back same."

"Well, okay then," Tate said, climbing into the Jeep with Laird for the ride to the bunkhouse. "Mister Tony. He's the boss."

* * *

It wasn't until dinner on the evening of the following day that Laird first encountered Tony Poe, the legendary CIA paramilitary officer who ran operations at the Long Tieng base. Tate knew him from previous SF encounters, but for Laird, this was a first.

Tony Poe, whose real name was Anthony Alexander Poshepny, was actually a Marine Corps veteran of World War II, most notable for his service in the battle for Iwo Jima - a month-long struggle that consumed thousands of lives. After the war and his discharge from the Marines, Poshepny drifted into an association with the Central Intelligence Agency as a paramilitary officer. He very soon found himself working with South Korean and Taiwanese commando trainees during that iteration of the new Cold War.

Now in Laos, *Tony Poe* had established a reputation for himself as a fearsome White warlord who sought to bring death and terror onto the Communist enemies. He allegedly sanctioned his indigenous warriors to inflict wild medieval savagery upon the enemy, Pathet Lao and North Vietnamese Army alike. This included the taking of ears and the severing of heads of the vanquished. He was idolized by his near-stone-aged warrior crew and was an ideal match for Vang Pao.

This was not the traditional American way of war. But maybe, some thought, it was the unacknowledged way of the new system of warfare.

Poe was waiting for them in the secluded dining area of the camp. The table had plates for three laid out. He took a sip of beer for a glass and rose up to greet them.

"Tate, you creaky asshole," he grinned, giving him a bearhug. "Thought I heard that you went to back to Hawaii after turning yourself inside out."

"That's a little bit exaggerated," Tate replied. "But yeah, I spent some time in Honolulu. Not on a beach, though. Shitbird." Motioning to Laird, he added, "And this is Jay. Our newest addition to the office. Comes from somewhere he calls Kansas."

"Jay," Poe said, shaking his hand with a tight grip. "I'm Tony. Welcome aboard. Take a seat."

In Laird's estimation, the personification of Poe did not match his near-demonic reputation in any sense. He was a chunky figure, pushing forty, with a receding hairline and an open smile.

"Vang Pao?" Tate asked. "Where's he at?"

Poe shook his head. "Here and gone again," he said. "Off to see another village of supporters. You missed him. He's as much a politician as a warrior these days."

"Well damn," Tate groused. "Would have liked to see him again."

As they seated themselves, a pair of young Hmong girls entered with jars of clear liquor. Pouring the rice spirits drink into their glasses next to the larger beer mugs, they nodded with smiles and respectfully backed out of the room.

Poe raised his glass of the rice liquor and proposed a brief toast.

"*Sat Cong*," he said. Kill the Cong. Death to the Communists. "Welcome aboard."

"*Sat Cong*," they repeated, knocking back the fiery liquid in single gulps.

That done, Poe reached for his beer mug once again. "By the way, your HOPPER guys are here," he announced. "Came in a few days ago. All five of them... Grim-faced little bastards," he pronounced. "I like 'em."

He was referring to the five-man team, led by the veteran Keej, who would soon be going North to attempt to kill the Cao Bang province chief. Plucked from the ranks of former street criminals, Keej was indeed a grim-faced little bastard. With a track record of controlled violence.

The two Hmong serving girls came back in with bowls of chicken, boiled white rice and assorted vegetables. Typical fare for the mountain people. They place the bowls in the center of the table and again quickly retreated.

At Poe's gesture, Laird began to spoon out some of the food to his plate. "The team is as ready to go as they ever will be," he said. "Launch tomorrow night?"

Poe shook his head. "Negative, Kansas. Not for at least the next three days. Bad weather up North near the drop site." He reached toward the community bowl. "Besides, Saturday the 13th is a full moon night. All the better for a drop."

"At least it's not a drop on Friday the 13th," Laird observed.

"The weather dictates," Tate agreed. "But it's not a good idea to keep a team on ice for very long once they're prepped and ready to go."

"No argument there," Poe said. "As far as I'm concerned, in three more days, they either launch on the mission or go back to Saigon and regroup."

"Okay," Laird said. "Three days. A lockdown or a killing."

SIXTEEN - HOPPER

Cao Bang Province
North Vietnam
October 1962

As forecast, the night of Saturday, October the 13th was a clear night replete with a full moon. The five-man HOPPER team, and all of their gear, kicked out of the VIAT plane on schedule over the Cao Bang province of North Vietnam.

Had they looked to the north as they plummeted through the night sky, the expanse of Communist China would have passed through their view. Preoccupied as they were however, none took advantage of the view.

Thankfully, the drop was uneventful, with the three members of the PROSPECT team on the ground to recover them. Within minutes, the newcomers were collected, bustled into the awaiting vehicles and taken to a preselected safe haven.

* * *

On the morning of the 16th, three days after the drop, the CIA team convened at the NVOB secure offices to do a status brief on the operation.

Jim Koval, looking tired and bleary-eyed, chaired the meeting. Tate, Laird and Sarpi rounded out the list of attendees.

"Okay, Jayhawk," Koval intoned. "You're the guy. Let's hear it."

"The HOPPER team went in as planned on the 13th," Laird began. "No hostile coverage seen. Certainly, no hostile action encountered. The aircraft departed the area after receiving a *team okay* signal from the ground."

"And now?" Sarpi asked, jotting down notes for his report to Headquarters.

"Now doing the final surveillance and rehearsal runs," Laird said.

The team was into the third phase of what was called the *Attack Cycle*. Target selection and initial surveillance had been completed. The action items were next.

"They are confirming what our PROSPECT guys already learned," Laird went on. "The target, Luong Hanh, seems to be damn near Germanic in his predictability... Goes to the office at the same time. Stays there all day. And then in the late afternoon, he picks up his girlfriend and they go for drinks at a sidewalk place in town."

"A sidewalk café in Communism?" Tate smirked.

"Like Orwell said, I guess that some animals are more equal than others."

"And that is where the operation will take place," Koval prompted.

"Right," Laird said.

"And, as I hear, the initial plan of an explosives attack is out," Koval continued.

"Right," Tate said, taking up the narrative. "Too risky in that environment. Too much chance of causing collateral damage."

"Like the girlfriend," Sarpi offered.

"Yeah," Laird said. "Like her."

"So, the other option?"

As Tate nodded, Laird continued. "Sniping. Mid-range. From a nearby building with a view of the café."

"Accompanied by an explosive charge set off down the street," Tate added. "As a distraction to aid in the escape."

"Vehicles?" Koval asked.

"The PROSPECT team obtained a pair of old Renault vans. Apparently, they resemble toasters on wheels. Beat up, but they run. And they fit in."

"Extraction plan?"

"Plan A, push east to the coast. Moving quick off the 'X' before they close the bridges over the Song Bang River. Water extraction," Laird said. "Plan B, go north to the Chinese border and cross into Guanxi Province. Go to ground and await recovery."

Koval nodded. "And Plan C?"

Tate shook his head. "There's no Plan C, Jim. This one is happening on the outer edges of our reach."

"Okay," Koval breathed. "Just one other thing. But a pretty big thing."

The others waited attentively.

"Last night, the Station received a Priority message from Langley," he began. "I know that you've probably been seeing some traffic about developments in Cuba."

"Not really our gig," Tate laughed. "Unless you're talking about old Fabian over at Carriage House."

"On Sunday, a U-2 did an overflight of an area in western Cuba, near San Cristobal... According to the analysts, they got photos of what they believe is a Soviet SS-14 missile site."

He was met with blank stares all around.

"SS-14," he repeated. "IRBM, an intermediate-range ballistic missile. Has a range of under 2,000 miles or so. Nuclear capable. And aimed at the United States."

"Well, I'll be shit," Tate snarled, his smile quickly fading. "That god-dammed Castro."

"Yeah," Koval agreed. "Kennedy is supposedly holding a strategy session today to come up with a response. Depending on Washington's reaction, we might all quickly become something of a sorry side-show over here."

* * *

On Friday, October 19th, the HOPPER team was set up in their lair and ready. Caught up in their own drama, the team was blissfully unaware of the potential of a nuclear exchange that was being discussed between JFK and his senior military planners that very day.

The team leader and designated shooter – Keej – was lying in wait on the third floor of the building facing Luong's favored cafe. Another member of the team was posted alongside of him to spot and assist. The other three team members were on the lower floors securing the exits and preparing the Renault get-away vehicle.

The members of the PROSPECT team were situated several blocks to the north of the site in preparation for the distraction exercise.

With the day's work done, Luong, his female partner and his security detail arrived at the expected location as usual. With Luong and his girlfriend settling into their favorite table on the corner of the café, two members of his detail dropped into their usual chairs at an adjoining table.

Keej shouldered his weapon as his target accepted his drink. The attractive woman at his side laughingly appeared to be sharing a story with him, likely recalling the day's events.

Luong's accustomed drink was a glass of Cointreau over ice. His partner ordered white wine. The security detail made do with water.

The weapon on Keej's shoulder was a Soviet-made *Dragunov*, or SVD, sniper rifle. It held a ten-round magazine of 7.62mm ammunition. The semi-automatic rifle also sported a mounted scope – an accessory that was hardly necessary at these distances.

Keej's team had accomplished the next two phases of the Attack Cycle: deployment to the attack site and target identification. What came next was foreordained.

Keej was lying prone on a table, well removed from the open window so as to preclude observation from the street below. As he peered through the scope, the reticles settled on the attractive face of Luong's girlfriend.

Releasing his breath, Keej shifted the focus from the woman to the face of the Province Chief, Luong Hanh. He dropped the point of aim to Luong's chest and squeezed the trigger. The first round impacted Luong's sternum. The second took him in the head.

The woman screamed in panic as the two bodyguards began to react in shock. Keej shifted his aim again and shot each man once.

The sudden pandemonium in the crowded street was accelerated by a pair of explosive blasts from a block away. That was the work of the PROSPECT team.

Keej and the others clambered down the back stairs to the awaiting Renault van to complete the next phase of the cycle – escape. The final step – exploitation of the act – would be left to others.

SEVENTEEN - MINERVA

NVOB – Saigon
October 29, 1962

The figure sitting in front of them what not exactly what the two CIA men had expected. Nevertheless, there he was - at their request - to assist with the preparation of the newly-minted MINERVA team.

For the past two months, Laird and Tate worked to train up MINERVA - a unit comprised of four Vietnamese agents - for their proposed operation into the denied area of Laos.

Whatever stress had been connected with the short-range preparation of a new team paled in comparison with the international events of the past week. An enormous amount of tension had been compressed into a relatively short period of time, leaving everyone close to emotional exhaustion.

The past seven days witnessed the President's decision and announcement to establish a blockade of Cuba. This was met with the Soviet challenge and withdrawal. It concluded with a hastily formed agreement to remove the offending missiles in return for a US promise not to invade the island.

The very day after the agreement, a U2 aircraft was shot down over Cuba, killing the pilot – a US Air Force officer. It was an action that threatened to re-escalate the confrontation.

Then just the day before, on Sunday the 28th, JFK and Khrushchev reached an accord - the process of which was unknown to the NVOB. The crisis had finally passed. Or so everyone hoped.

And while the HOPPER operation appeared to have been a success, the team went dark two days after the assassination. Their fate remained unknown to the NVOB. Yet another mystery.

The objective of the operation was to securely insert a team into Laos. It was there, in supposedly neutral territory, that the North Vietnamese had constructed a heavily used logistics channel from the North down into South Vietnam. It was called the *Ho Chi Minh Trail* - in honor of the Communist leader in Hanoi. Established in the late 1950s, the Trail was by then running day and night, steadily dispatching troops and material into the combat zone.

Once along the Trail in the jungle, the members of MINERVA were to proceed to a specific spot where intelligence had identified a physical communications junction. There, they would install a tap on the line that would begin to surreptitiously monitor and record North Vietnamese military communications.

The four team members, Toan, Lanh, Bao and Quan, were each technically adept young men with no military experience. All came from urban backgrounds, having been recruited from the environs of Saigon. And that was the problem.

Middle-class boys, all four came from good families and were reliably committed to the anti-Communist cause. None, however, had spent any time to speak of in the rural environment. Their milieu was the school campus, classrooms, coffee houses and the hotels - not the damp undergrowth of the forests that awaited them in Laos.

And that was where the NVOB's guest came in.

The stranger was a Caucasian American. Clad in blue jeans and a short-sleeved plaid shirt, he was a lanky figure in civilian clothing with sun-bleached reddish-blonde hair and a bushy mustache.

To the Agency men, he looked more like a ruddy, hard-boned construction worker than anything else. In actuality, he was an experienced American Navy NCO - an E-7 Chief Petty Officer - named Thad.

Until a year or so ago, Thad had been a career Frogman - a member of the Underwater Demolitions Teams. He was now part of the newly-formed US Navy SEAL organization. He was in Vietnam as part of the training project they were conducting for their Vietnamese SEAL counterparts, the LDNN.

Thad listened attentively as Laird and Tate briefed him as to the mission of the MINERVA team.

"Sounds good to me," he drawled at last. "Just the same, where do I fit into all of this, uh, subterfuge?"

"Quality control," Laird said. "I guess you could say."

"Quality control?" Thad echoed.

"Our boys are technically ready to go," Tate began. "So far as it goes... Some might say that they are smart and capable, but still just Saigon Cowboys."

"But we want to give them a realistic final exercise," Laird added. "Along with some practical training... Drop them off in the hinterlands for about a week or so. Let them place a tap, unannounced, on an actual ARVN commo line. And face the possibility of a little real danger on the ground. Courtesy of the VC."

"The VC, maybe," Tate qualified.

"And so, you are looking for a babysitter," Thad said.

"More of an experienced evaluator, I would say," Tate observed. "Someone who can help put them through their paces out in the wild."

"Okay," Thad said. "But I'm a practitioner - not a linguist. How do I communicate with these guys?"

"They all speak English," Tate assured him. "Well enough anyhow."

Thad nodded. "And where are you thinking about doing this exercise?"

"An area that you are already familiar with," Laird answered, shifting in his chair. "The *Rung Sat* Special Zone."

The Rung Sat was a marshy area some twenty miles southeast of Saigon comprising nearly five hundred square miles of territory. Also known as the *Forest of the Assassins*, it was an apt target area bordering on the South China Sea. As the CIA knew, the SEALs were already active in the swamp, training the LDNN.

The Viet Cong adversaries were also active in the same area. But not for training.

"Okay," Thad agreed. "When are we doing this?"

EIGHTEEN - WANDERING SOULS

**Rung Sat Special Zone
South Vietnam
November 7, 1962**

Several days after the meeting at the NVOB, an American Army UH-1B helicopter carried the MINERVA team, with its freshly assigned SEAL evaluator, deep into the Rung Sat Special Zone. Pausing only to do a quick off-load into the wetlands, the Huey quickly bounced back into the air. The aircraft pivoted 180 degrees in a low hover, nosed down and flew away, leaving the five heavily burdened men to their own resources.

As planned, the actual MINERVA operation would involve a low-level parachute jump into an area within range of the Ho Chi Minh Trail. For training purposes however, the managers at the NVOB decided not to risk broken legs or ankles at this late date in the game. It was decided that a helo insertion would suffice for the purposes of the exercise.

The team was purposely dropped at a point that would require several days of movement through the difficult terrain in order to reach an unsuspecting ARVN commo site. Their tactical and woodland skills would be assessed and honed during that time.

As always, Thad was wearing his lucky, soft brimmed boonie hat. Tucked under his arm was a Belgian-made FN/FAL battle rifle with a folding stock. As he stepped off the skid and onto the swampy ground, he was humping a rucksack solidly packed with food, water, a radio, spare batteries and ammunition.

Thick lines of green and brown camouflage war paint streaked his face. It was a trademark that would later cause the Viet Cong to refer to their American SEAL foes as *the men with green faces*.

Despite his fearsome presence, Thad was not there to run the operation. That job was left to the MINERVA team leader, Toan. At age twenty-eight, Toan was the oldest of the agent group. Thad was only to observe and report their decisions and actions. And when needed, serve as a tactical coach.

For the first several days in the swamp, all went well. The team adapted reasonably to the harsh environment. From Thad's perspective, they showed good morale, security awareness and movement discipline.

On their third day in the Zone, the team reached the site of the ARVN commo line. With Toan, Lanh and Quan providing security, Bao, the most technically proficient member, moved forward to affix the technical tap onto the communications node.

As Bao worked his magic in the darkness, the team members nervously held their security positions around the site. The threat was posed not only by hostile random VC patrols but by the unwitting, and possibly trigger-happy, soldiers of the ARVN who might stumble by as well.

The job done, Bao pulled back to link up with Thad and the team. Together, they fell back to a pre-arranged rally site and made contact with the NVOB in Saigon. Minutes later, a return message from NVOB assured them that the tap was live and transmitting properly.

So far, so good.

* * *

The weather took a turn for the worse that night. As the clouded afternoon skies blackened into night, they produced gusts of wind and sporadic bursts of rain.

As per the SOP, Toan found a suitable laying up point on a dry patch of land for resting overnight. He set an alternating watch schedule between the team members, with three resting and one keeping watch. Satisfied with the arrangements, Toan authorized those not on watch to wrap themselves in their ponchos and turn in for such sleep as was possible.

Sometime later, Thad stirred himself awake. The rain had stopped, but the wind continued to rustle through the treetops. That, combined with the muted chattering of the MINERVA teammates, had roused him from his slumber.

Despite the lack of rain, the wind velocity was increasing. As it continued, it took little imagination to hear the noise interspersed with a low keening sound. With little imagination, one could say that it was comprised of a series of unintelligible voices, softly moaning in unison.

Even in the darkness, Thad could sense the jittery state of mind of the Vietnamese team. All were now alert and wide-eyed, scanning their perimeter for threats. Spiritual or otherwise.

No believer in the paranormal, Thad thumbed off the safety of his FN/FAL rifle and awaited what he assumed to be the possible approach of an errant VC patrol. He pulled a spare ammo magazine out of its canvas pouch and carefully placed it next to the gun. Lying prone in his water-soaked clothing, he relied more on his senses of hearing and smell rather than sight.

The noises intensified, though the wind velocity did not. As he listened, even the experienced SEAL began to hear what appeared to be strains of discordant musical notes floating among the muted rustling of voices.

After twenty or so tense minutes, the environment settled back into its normal state. As the night itself seemed to relax, so did the team.

It took the better part of an hour for Thad to lapse back into a confused and restless sleep.

* * *

As dawn broke, Thad huddled with Toan. They quietly conferring as to the events of the previous evening.

"What was all that shit about last night?" Thad whispered as they breakfasted over their cold rations. The SEAL advisor was careful to avoid being overheard by the other three team members as he spooned into his C-ration can of food.

"Truthfully, I don't know," Toan muttered. "But the men think it could have been spirits... The spirits of the dead."

"Spirits?" Thad repeated. "You mean as in ghosts?"

Toan shrugged, unscrewing the cap of his canteen. "I don't know what your people believe in the West," he said, taking a swig of tepid water. "But over here, we believe in the concepts of a good death and a bad death."

Thad nodded and kept eating. "Okay."

"To die a good death - *Chet Nha,* as we call it - is to die at home," Toan explained. "To die amid one's family and loved ones. If that is the case, one's spirit can rest at peace for eternity."

"And the bad death?" Thad prompted.

"That is *Chet Duong*... The bad death is the death in the street, so to say. The death far from your ancestral homelands. A violent death, even worse."

"Like a death in war, in other words?"

"Yes," Toan agreed. "Such unfortunates are called *Wandering Souls*. They are lost. They are stumbling about the world of people confused and in pain. They are fated to do this forever. You understand this? Forever? Until the end of time."

"Gotta say, though," Thad grimaced. "Sounds a little odd to me."

"With respect, Thad, your Santa Claus sounds a little odd to me too," Toan retorted softly.

Thad nodded. "I get it."

***

That evening the team settled into their next overnight point. It followed a full day of steadily slogging towards their designated pick-up location. As they moved through the difficult terrain, Thad noted that both their movement and Toan's control of the team were tactically sound.

In his opinion, they were good to go. Mission capable.

Overhead, the night sky was again black and cloud-covered, yet there was thankfully no rain.

Still, as the hours progressed, the wind velocity slowly yet steadily increased. Try as he might, Thad was unable to force himself into sleep.

An hour or two past midnight, he awoke from a light doze. Whether the distraction was the patter of raindrops splattering on his shoulders or the troubling ambient noise was uncertain. The wind was again singing through the upper branches of the trees.

Coming fully conscious, Thad became aware of vocalizations that were similar to those of the previous evening. Now on alert, he carefully unwound himself from the confines of his poncho. He extended the folded stock of his FAL/FN and pulled it closer into his body.

Even without seeing them, he sensed that the four Vietnamese men were also awake and tensely on alert.

Bao and Lanh began to mumble quietly to each other as the sounds again assumed the pitch of musical, whining voices.

Whether it was the increasing movement of the wind or his own imagination, Thad could not tell.

Truthfully, he was beginning to believe that he was spending too much time in the woods with his superstitious Vietnamese colleagues. He, too, was hearing the undecipherable voices.

For several minutes the Rung Sat lapsed into silence, save for the sounds of the rain splattering onto the foliage. As Thad scanned the darkness, his attention was drawn to a faint blue light far off to their left flank.

Incredulously, the misty light appeared to be slowly approaching them, spreading its wings both left and right as it did so. All the while, the musical voices overhead increased in their intensity.

Toan uttered a soft, shushing noise as his team members began audibly mumbling their fearful discomfort.

Thad didn't know what he was witnessing, but he found it to be beyond belief that the VC, familiar as he was with their tactics, could be so blatant in their movements. Whatever it was, it was not subtle. If anything, it was broadcasting its presence.

The blue light began to fade. While doing so, a dimly-lit rainbow effect glimmered. Although he had never seen them in person, it reminded Thad of images of the Northern Lights.

The crack of a nearby weapon startled him. A rattle of semi-automatic gunfire followed as the frightened MINERVA team members opened up on the light show.

"Cease fire! Cease fire!" Thad commanded, cursing softly to himself.

Toan repeated the command in Vietnamese for added effect.

As the noise of the gunfire died away, so did the mysterious lights. Likewise, the oddly melodic sounds expired, and the rain swept back in.

"Anyone have a target?"

There was no response.

"Goddammit," Thad muttered, scrambling to his feet. "Huddle up on me... Now!" he said.

The five men quickly gathered into a quick, kneeling huddle. "Okay, listen up", Thad began tightly. "That shooting was unnecessary. Irresponsible. If there's any VC in the area, we're damn good and well compromised now."

"Sorry..." one of the men began.

"No time for that," Thad interrupted. "Toan, we need to move out of here," he commanded. "We'll go southwest - compass heading of 230 degrees. I'll take point. You bring up the rear."

"Yes, sir," Toan agreed.

"Linh," Thad continued, touching the man on his shoulder. "You stay right behind me and keep the pace count, so we know how far we're traveling."

"Yes, sir," Linh replied.

"Keep it tight. No stragglers." The men nodded their understanding.

"Questions?"

There were none.

"Good. Grab your shit, and let's go."

Thad heaved his rucksack up onto his shoulders and pulled out a lensatic compass. Once they were some distance away from the site, he would call into the NVOB and request helo extraction at first light - location to be determined.

And with that, the five men quickly trekked away from their lay-up site, the majority of them wide-eyed and shaken.

* * *

Koval glanced up from the written report, frowning in disbelief. Thad, Laird and Tate sat about the NVOB conference table. The air conditioner rattled softly in the background.

"So, what *did* they see out there?" Koval asked.

"They saw lights. Heard music. Voices, maybe," Thad said.

"But no VC?"

"Not that I ever saw."

"Any return fire after the shooting incident?"

"None."

"And no further incidents on the way to the extraction point?"

"Nothing... We had enough adventure for the night."

Koval dropped the report on the table. "What did *you* see?"

Thad hesitated, gathering his thoughts. "I did see those glimmering bluish lights that they talked about in the report."

"And the musical voices?" Laird prompted.

Thad shrugged. "Nature can play with your senses out there in the elements. Screw around with your head... I heard the wind and rain moving through the branches. Music? Not so sure."

"Lights could have been coming from Saigon," Laird speculated. "Reflected off the bottoms of those rainclouds, maybe."

"That far out in the middle of the Rung Sat?" Thad scoffed. "Not so much."

"Swamp gas?" Tate offered. "Phosphorous gases? They could luminate."

"I'm not an authority on that," the SEAL said. "But I doubt it."

"Maybe the lights coming from a nearby village?" Laird pursued, following his theme.

Thad shifted in his chair. "You ever see a Viet village all lit up in blue?" he challenged. "Me neither."

"Well, the exercise was still largely successful," Tate said. "The tap on the ARVN line was good. Still transmitting."

"We'll pass the take to the Tech Unit," Koval said. "For as long as it lasts. See what they are saying about things."

"But as far as the actual mission goes..." Laird began.

"They're refusing the mission," Thad interrupted again. "Thought you already knew that."

"Refusing?"

Thad nodded. "Last thing Toan told me after the debrief. They aren't going."

"They're afraid to go up on the Trail now?" Koval asked, grim-faced.

The SEAL shook his head. "Not so much the Trail... They're afraid of whatever it is that's in those woods."

The three CIA men looked at each other in silence.

Sighing, Koval reached over and retrieved the typed report. He uncapped a felt-tipped Flair marker and drew a red line through the word *MINERVA*.

"Well shit," he muttered.

NINETEEN - CROWN COLONY

Hong Kong
December 9, 1962

It was their last day on the island. Tomorrow was back to the war.

Tuyet's face beamed as she took in the scenic view from Victoria Peak. They were some 1,300 feet above sea level. Down below were the towering buildings of the Central District.

Across Victoria Harbor to the north was Kowloon. It was the geographically larger part of the territory that was physically linked to the mainland of Communist China.

They were not in Communist China, however. They were in Hong Kong. The *British Crown Colony* of Hong Kong.

The colony was considered to be one of the four "*Asian Tigers,*" the others being South Korea, Taiwan and Singapore. It had been ravaged earlier in the year by Hurricane Wanda, killing over 400 people. But it appeared to have recovered and was back to its normal business – that of business.

Laird was looking appreciatively at Tuyet, as opposed to the fabled touristic view down below. Previously he had requested and obtained the permission of the Station to take a long weekend in Hong Kong, along with Tuyet. It had been a relaxing version of a brief R&R for them both.

The previous day they had taken a boat from Hong Kong over to the neighboring Portuguese colony of Macau. Touted as the *Monte Carlo of the East*, Macau had been a possession of Portugal since the 16th century. It has been a mecca of gambling since the 1850s.

While enjoying the intimacies of their brief romantic get-away in Hong Kong, Laird could not shake the news that hit the Saigon Station in the days before their departure.

In late November, the Democratic Senate Majority Leader, Mike Mansfield of Montana, led a bipartisan Congressional fact-finding mission to Vietnam. The results of his findings were not favorable to the policies of the Administration.

On the second of December Senator Mansfield released a public statement that was to be the first of a critical nature, by a ranking US political official of American policy in Vietnam.

Mansfield noted that the US Government had channeled 2 billion dollars' worth of aid into South Vietnam over the course of the past seven years. This vast expenditure of public funds, he said, accomplished nothing. In effect, a fortune had been squandered on what he perceived to be a lost cause.

Mansfield's remedy called for a US pull-out from Vietnam. Sooner rather than later.

The day after Mansfield's announcement, in a distinctly non-public communique, the Director of the State Department's Bureau of Intelligence and Research (INR), Roger Hillsman, sent a Top-Secret memorandum to the Secretary of State, Dean Rusk.

In the memorandum, Hillsman posited that the regime of President Diem maintained that the South Vietnamese government was being successful in its efforts and had turned the tide on the insurgency in the country. Hillman's memo did nothing to discount Mansfield. In his view, Diem was being premature. The US aid to the South Vietnamese, he said, had done nothing more than slow the deterioration against the Communist onslaught.

Back to the war indeed.

TWENTY - DESPEDIDA

Saigon, South Vietnam
Mid-December 1962

It was late in the afternoon. The light was fading, as was the heat of the day. Laird, Tate and Sarpi were lounging around a metal table in the enclosed courtyard of the NVOB building, sharing beer and cigars. They were awaiting the arrival of Jim Koval, who was still busy in the office.

Once Koval arrived, they would be adjourning to the home of a senior Station officer. The latter was hosting a *despedida*, or a farewell, going away party, for Chief of Station Bill Colby. The host, having recently served in Central America, glommed onto the Spanish term for his event. A *despedida* in Southeast Asia? Indeed, why not?

As previously announced, Colby was leaving Vietnam to assume the post of Director of the Far East Division at CIA headquarters in Langley. He was leaving behind a program – and a war – that was far from showing promise, despite all of the sacrifices.

"I hear that we're going to be taking possession of a couple Nasties within a month or so," Tate announced, taking a gulp of beer from his bottle. "Should be useful for the maritime operations."

Laird cocked an eyebrow. "Nasties being what?"

"*Nasty*. A term for Norwegian-built combat patrol boats, son," Tate replied. "Where've you been? They come armed with both 40 and 80 mike-mike guns, plus an optional mortal tube or a fifty cal. They're fast too. Better than the SWIFT boats that the maritime teams have been using. Can inflict some mean shit. Damn."

"Okay, okay," Laird said, holding up a hand. "Nasties. I'm a fan."

"Interesting report today from Hanoi via Langley," Sarpi chimed in. "Not to change the subject."

"Do tell," Tate said.

"Their Politburo met earlier this month. It appears that they are concerned about the mobility advantage of the American advisors and ARVN troops. Right now, it looks insurmountable to them."

"But I'm sure they'll do their damndest," Tate observed.

"Right. They're also concerned about the small numbers of what they call liberated zones here in the South. They see the Strategic Hamlet Program as an obstruction that needs to be overcome. They've ordered a military construction unit to work on improving the logistics road into the South. The Ho Chi Minh Trail"

Tate shook his head. "We should be bombing the living shit out of an improved high-speed supply route like that."

He reached into a cooler by their feet and produced three more chilled bottles of Thai *Singha* beer. "Time for one more till the Boss gets down here, I'm thinking."

He popped off the caps with a church-key and clinked bottles with the other two.

"A hail and farewell," Laird observed. "Out with the old, in with the new."

"Watch that *old* shit, brother," Tate cautioned.

"Anyhow," Laird continued. "Anyone know anything about the new guy?"

"John Richardson," Sarpi said. "Better known as Jocko. He's been around for twenty or so years. Joined the club back when it was called the Strategic Services Unit. Just after the OSS and before becoming the Agency. Served in Austria, Greece, the Philippines... Koval knows him."

"Knows him how?" Laird pressed.

Sarpi took a swig of his beer. "Remember me telling you about Koval and AERODYNAMIC, back in the day? Ferrying agents into the Ukraine and all that?"

"I do."

"And you'll recall me telling you about a Balkans operation called VALUABLE FIEND. Trying to do the same thing in Albania."

"Yes."

"Well, that's the connection. Koval was working for Richardson in '54. Jocko was then a regional director in Langley. He's the guy who killed off FIEND as a project."

"And now off he goes to Saigon," Tate said. "To see how it's working on the ground."

"Well, he's inheriting a handful," Sarpi said. "We have about eleven thousand US advisors here working with the ARVN. Supporting the Diem regime. The same people who've been running the place since '55. Corrupt as hell and not getting any better. Resisting all calls for reforms. The Strategic Hamlet

Program is pissing off everyone in the countryside... How am I doing?"

"So, other than that..." Tate said.

"Other than that," Sarpi said. "Here comes our Jimbo. Off to the party."

TWENTY-ONE - ENCOUNTER AT AP BAC

Ap Bac, South Vietnam
January 2, 1963

The US Army's communications intercept group - the Army Security Agency, or ASA - was one of the initial units that had been thrown into the Vietnam conflict. One of ASA's early cover names in-country had been that of the *Radio Research Unit*.

In point of fact, the first American combat death in Vietnam was that of an ASA soldier. He was Army Specialist 4th Class James T. Davis, a Tennessee native and a Direction-Finding Operator. Davis was killed in December of 1961 in an ambush near an old French military post called Cau Xang.

In late December of 1962, the ASA detected the presence of a radio transmitter. That transmitter was associated with a significant body of Communist forces in the South. Specifically, it was traced to the 261st and 514th VC battalions. The location of the transmitter was placed in the area of Ap Bac, in Dinh Tuong province. It was some forty miles southwest of Saigon in the Mekong Delta region.

In tactical terms, the locale was not ideal for military operations. Rice paddies and canals crisscrossed the area. The vegetation favored the defensive, serving to hamper both movement and observation.

The find, however, was a welcomed discovery. Continually frustrated by the elusive hit and run tactics of the Viet Cong, both the ARVN commanders and especially their American advisors had long sought a chance to pin down the enemy in a standing set-piece battle. It seemed as though that opportunity had finally presented itself.

On the morning of Wednesday, January 2nd, the ARVN forces sallied out against the enemy. What they encountered turned out to be a force of approximately 320 VC soldiers who were planted in unexpectedly well-prepared defensive positions.

Unbeknownst to the ARVN, however, their tactical plans had already been leaked to the enemy. The source was a well-placed Communist spy in Saigon working as a journalist named Pham Xuan An. Ironically the agent, who occasionally worked for a New

York newspaper, was a favorite of the American journalists working in-country.

The information that Pham provided forewarned the Viet Cong and enabled them to prepare for the coming assault. His advice included the employment of captured heavy machine guns, which were to be used to great effect that day.

The battle kicked off with the introduction of elements of the ARVN's 7th Infantry Division, 11th Infantry Regiment and two Civil Guards battalions. Their objectives were the twin hamlets of Ap Bac and Ap Tan Thoi. Circling overhead in a fixed-wing L-19 Bird Dog spotter plane was the senior American advisor to the 7th Infantry, Lieutenant Colonel John Paul Vann.

Vann had a reputation for being a forceful, aggressive, and occasionally abrasive officer. As an experienced advisor, one of his ongoing concerns was the reluctance of the ARVN commanders to hit the enemy and accept the requisite combat casualties. In fact, there was an official directive from President Diem that his commanders were to keep combat casualties to a minimum while inflicting the maximum of causalities upon the enemy.

Diem also had a policy of the promotions of ARVN officers – and sometimes even NCOs – based upon their familial relationships and political reliability, as opposed to their professional competency.

As Vann was well aware, the ARVN strategy tended to favor the safety of stand-off attacks from rockets and artillery rounds. While potentially effective, despite American attempts to encourage discretion, they also inflicted numbers of wounded and dead upon the very same villagers that they desired to attract to the government's side. As he understood it, his duty was to push the ARVN commanders into a more aggressive posture.

Upon hearing the sound of approaching land vehicles and aircraft early in the morning, the VC scrambled to their prepared fighting positions. Before much longer, a large force of helicopters came into view over the horizon. They were carrying a battalion of the ARVN 11th Infantry into the action.

As the engagement began, the ARVN commander committed the first of the two Civil Guards battalions. The latter were uniformed and lightly armed groups that were more closely aligned to police than military formations. When they became pinned down by enemy fire, the commander refused to deploy the second battalion to assist the first. The battle was quickly showing signs of becoming a stalemate.

After several hours of failed attempts to break the VC line, a decision was made to punch through with mechanized troops in the form of M-113 armored personnel carriers, or APCs. Unfortunately, as the APCs pushed forward, they quickly became bogged down in the mud and water of the rice paddy canals. Another attack stalled.

From overhead, Vann attempted to assert control by having a ground-based US advisor divert troops for a rescue. This effort failed when the ground advisor's ARVN partner refused, stating that he did not take orders from Americans.

In the late afternoon, as the battle struggled along without success, the senior ARVN commander eventually relented to Vann's entreaties and ordered the parachute drop of 300 soldiers of his 8th Airborne Battalion. By miscue, however, when the battalion jumped, they hit ground directly in front of the VC positions instead of landing behind the cover of the APCs, as had been the plan. Despite taking heavy fire, the paratroopers attempted several attacks against the VC positions. Failing to reach the defending VC, they became what is described as *combat ineffective*.

With the light of day fading, the VC commander feared encirclement and ordered a withdrawal. His troops pulled out of their positions in an orderly manner, taking their dead and wounded along with them as best they could.

Despite overwhelming South Vietnamese numbers, after some 15 hours of fighting, the VC was able to successfully break contact with the ARVN and slip away once again.

The results of the day's action were eighteen VC killed and thirty-nine wounded. On the other hand, an estimated eighty ARVN soldiers were killed, with a hundred wounded. Three Americans lost their lives as well. Five US helicopters were downed in the course of the fighting, adding to the overall cost in men and material.

The following morning, with the enemy long gone, the ARVN troops could advance onto the objective unopposed. This enabled South Vietnamese officials to claim a battlefield success. In the aftermath of the battle, more senior US commanders were also quick to claim a victory for their South Vietnamese allies.

An on-site American reporter, however, asked a US Brigadier General, Robert York, to explain what had happened on the battlefield.

"What the hell does it look like boy?" York exclaimed in frustration. "They got away. That's what happened!"

The senior US advisor, LTC Vann, reputedly observed of the ARVN that "It was a damn miserable performance, just like it always is."

"These people won't listen," Vann continued. "They make the same goddamn mistakes over and over again in the same way."

Following the engagement, there was a consensus in Washington that the Diem government was unable to cope with the insurgency even as close to the capital as that in the Mekong Delta region. One review stated that that the ARVN was rife with poor morale and poor leadership.

As a result, the US authorities decided that - going forward, it would be *American* troops, not their South Vietnamese allies – who would have to carry the fight to the enemy.

TWENTY-TWO - SOTU

Washington, DC
January 14, 1963

Washington, DC. Monday, the 14th of January.

It was a typically cold day in Washington. The afternoon temperatures hovered at the freezing point. By nightfall, the temperatures had dropped even further. And evening was when the motorcade was moving. The Secret Service detail was securely transporting the President from the White House, over Pennsylvania Avenue, and up to his Capitol Hill destination.

As planned and expected, the advance agents of the Secret Service, along with the uniformed officers of the Capitol Police, met the motorcade as it rolled to a stop under the east portico of the historic building. The President, accompanied by the First Lady, exited the armored limousine into the cold night air and followed the agents up the steps and into the building.

He was at the Capitol for an annual political event – the State of the Union Address, otherwise known to the press as the *SOTU*. It was to be John F. Kennedy's third such address to a joint session of Congress. And, as it happened, it was to be his last.

The assemblage, consisting of both houses of Congress, the military chieftains, the justices of the Supreme Court and other dignitaries, stood and applauded as the President entered the chamber and made his way to the podium.

The President paused at the podium to accept and acknowledge the applause. Vice President Lyndon Johnson and Speaker John McCormack looked on from their places behind him. The First Lady, Jacqueline Bouvier Kennedy and her guests beamed down approvingly from the gallery.

The applause gradually subsided, allowing the President to launch into his prepared remarks. He began by noting that he had assumed the Presidency some hundred weeks earlier. As then, pledging then no easy answers, he only offered *"toil and dedication."*

As the event progressed, President Kennedy delivered his address with smooth and practiced professionalism. He hit a number of high points during the course of his speech. Among them was his recognition of twenty-two months of what he termed as uninterrupted economic recovery, with the recession well behind.

On top of that, he called for a substantial reduction of federal income taxes, which he said were too heavy a drag on private purchasing power and prospects for employment. Likewise, JFK pushed for a reduction in corporate taxes, for much the same reasons.

Regarding international affairs, the President offered the following comments:

"In the world beyond our borders, steady progress has been made in building a world of order. The people of West Berlin remain both free and secure. A settlement, though still precarious, has been reached in Laos. *The spearpoint of aggression has been blunted in Vietnam.* The end of agony may be in sight in the Congo. The doctrine of troika is dead. And, while danger continues, a deadly threat has been removed in Cuba."

In truth, on that January day, those on the ground knew that the spearpoint of aggression in Vietnam was far from being blunted.

TWENTY-THREE - SPECIAL ACTION

Saigon, South Vietnam
January 17, 1963

It was mid-morning on a Thursday. The traffic flow in downtown Saigon was congested, as usual. XL and Laird traveled in a sedan, making their way slowly to the SEPES compound for the weekly liaison meeting.

Despite the morning haze, Laird was wearing a pair of aviator-style sunglasses. All the better to present a cool appearance to the onlookers. The sunglasses were hardly necessary, however, as the windows of the sedan were so heavily shaded as to render the vehicle's glass to be nearly opaque.

As was customary, his bodyguard Xiao Lin, or XL, was driving the vehicle and smoothly maneuvering it through the thickening city traffic. In keeping with his usual practice, XL kept his favored weapon, a Swedish-K submachine gun, in the vehicle. It was wedged in tight to the seat, next to his right leg.

Loath to appear as a stereotypical, privileged Western colonialist, Laird eschewed the chauffeured rear seat of the car and was again riding in the right front seat, next to XL.

In terms of weaponry, Laird had a government-issued Colt .45 semiautomatic pistol with him. However, knowing that the SEPES people were often hinky about foreigners carrying weapons into their building, the gun was resting in the car's glove box. It was a firearm that he had never actually used, aside from qualifying on the range in basic and pre-deployment training. Out of sight, out of mind. Therefore, peace of mind for one and all.

Laird knew that there would be no passing meeting with Tuyet today. She was out of the city, spending a few days upcountry in Bien Hoa with her parents and siblings. As planned, that day's meeting would consist of an exchange of current intelligence material, followed by an on-site lunch and then a return to the NVOB compound.

While approaching the final turn toward their destination, a bicycle towing a rickety, wheeled cart gradually made its way up and alongside of them. A jittery, rail-thin teenaged boy operated the bike. The boy quickly glanced at the sedan and began to peddle a bit harder to move ahead of them.

Seconds later, the boy then abruptly swerved the bike and cart combination in front of the sedan and jerked the bike to a jangling stop. Even as XL slammed on the brakes to avoid an accident, the teenager jumped off of the bike and scampered away, leaving his vehicle in place.

"Asshole!" Laird blurted, bracing himself against the dashboard with one hand.

As Laird turned his attention back from the teenager to the cart in front of them, he noticed that a whiff of vaporous smoke was drifting out of it.

"Christ Almighty!" he exclaimed, recognizing the danger. He instinctively dropped onto the seat under the dash.

Scant moments later, the wooden cart exploded with a bright flash and a muted roar. At once, the sedan's hood was twisted apart and blown upward while the windshield crashed into the passenger compartment.

Outside of the vehicle, there were shrieks of pain and panic as the people on the street reacted to the blast.

After a few seconds, a dazed and bloodied XL pushed open his door and clambered out of the sedan, dragging the Swedish-K along with him. The first thing XL saw was the teenaged bike rider. He had turned and was coming back toward the crippled sedan at a gallop. The boy had a gun in his hand. And he was firing.

The first bullet he fired pranged off of the misshapen hood of the car. The next two shots hit XL in the torso. Yet another caught him in the upper thigh.

Sagging painfully against the frame of the car, XL leveled the Swedish-K at his boyish assailant and hammered him with a spray of hot 9mm rounds on full automatic.

That ended that particular gunfight.

Meanwhile, it took Laird another few seconds to regain his senses. His ears were ringing and blood from cuts on his head was flowing down his face, partially blinding him.

Acting primarily on instinct, he fumbled into the glove compartment for the Colt pistol. Simultaneously, rounds from a new direction began impacting into the seat behind him; the seat that he should have been occupying, as the chauffeured dignitary.

Painfully kicking his door open, Laird caught sight of the second attacker, and the latter of him. The second shooter had been tunnel-visioned on the rear of the sedan, where the VIP passenger would normally be sitting. Realizing his error, the new shooter began to swivel the muzzle of his revolver in Laird's direction.

At once, Laird quickly pushed the Colt forward in a two-handed grip. No focused aim on a front sight picture, as he had been taught at The Farm. Point shooting only.

He quickly pulled the trigger twice. The first round missed his target, sparking off of the bricks of a nearby building. The second round hit the teenager squarely in the chest, crumpling him to the sidewalk.

Laird pushed himself up and out of the car and fired three more times into the attacker's body as he did so. Satisfied with the effect but unsteady, he then turned to scan the area for additional threats.

In retrospect, he did not sense any recoil or appreciable noise from the high-powered pistol.

Panting, Laird paused while trying to assess the situation for additional threats. Blood smeared his face, causing his right eye to close. Absently, he touched at a gash in his head, coming away with yet more blood.

How many shots did he have left in the gun, he wondered? Two? Three?

Dimly, he recalled that there was a spare magazine for the Colt in the glove box. If he could get to it.

Laird's ears were ringing. Nevertheless, he could discern a din of discordant shouts, screams and the sounds of people fleeing the scene. He was faintly aware of the bodies of a couple of civilians scattered in front of the sedan. They were moaning and bleeding out.

He dropped back against the frame of the sedan's door and slumped into a sitting position on the street. The fingers of his left hand were beginning to tremble. Signs of shock, he surmised.

Oddly wearied, Laird could sense the small crackle of flames and the smell of burning rubber coming from the engine and the front tires. From the distance came the shrill sirens of approaching MP jeeps.

* * *

Later that day Koval and Sarpi met with the new COS, Jocko Richardson, and his deputy, the DCOS, at his office in the Saigon Station. The afternoon had been filled with a series of emergency meetings and priority cables going back and forth from the Station and the Headquarters in Langley. Richardson had been engaged in a conference offsite and was a bit out of the loop.

"And so," the COS said, opening the session. "Just to clarify the issue. Exactly who of our people were involved in this?"

"Jay Laird," Koval answered. "He's fairly new. A first-tour officer. And his local national bodyguard and driver, Xiao Lin. Ethnic Chinese. They were both taken to the ER over at the Naval Hospital."

"And what's their condition?"

"Laird took a handful of shrapnel and glass in the face," Koval said. "Dammed lucky that he didn't lose an eye when that windshield imploded... In all likelihood, he won't be quite as pretty as before, but he'll pull through."

There was a moment of reflective silence at that report.

"Thankfully, the bomb maker, whoever he is, was fairly inept," Sarpi interjected. "The device went off. But not with the force that it should have had."

"Thank God for that at least," Richardson said. "And the bodyguard?"

"XL," Koval shook his head ruefully. "Aside from the blast, he was shot three times. Right now, he's in intensive care. They aren't sure that he will make it. The odds aren't really in his favor."

"Obviously, the family will be compensated if he passes," Richardson said.

The DCOS nodded affirmatively.

The COS frowned. "What exactly happened? Did they know they were hitting an Agency vehicle? Do we know? What's next?"

"Ambush. On their way to a planned liaison meeting," Koval replied. "By what we think was the work of one of the VC urban sapper teams."

"Definitely a VC urban sapper unit," the DCOS said. "Our liaison partners were able to identify one of the two bodies that were left on the scene. He's a member of one of their so-called Special Action Teams. Specifically, Commando Unit 65."

"Urban sappers," Richardson repeated.

"Right," the DCOS continued. We estimate that five such teams are active here in Saigon. Enumerated as teams 65, 66, 67, 69 and 159."

"Well, at least one of them is gone now," Richardson said.

"Doubt it, sir," Koval said. "They'll probably reconstitute it pretty damn fast."

"These teams usually operate in three-man cells," the DCOS went on. "We've accounted for two of them. The third member – if there is a third member – probably hauled ass out of there."

"That's what I would've done," Sarpi quipped, earning himself a cocked eyebrow from the DCOS.

"So, these sappers," Richardson said. "How could they know that that Laird was Agency? That he had a meeting with our SEPES counterparts?"

"Hard to say at this point," the DCOS said, glancing at Koval. "Our CI shop is looking into any potential issues at the NVOB."

Koval leaned back in his chair and crossed his legs. "Sir, our operation is tight... I'm not saying that we can't be penetrated," he said. "But let's be real. This is Saigon. The VC has this place plastered with informants. They know what SEPES is. In fact, they would be criminally negligent if they weren't keeping watch on the place. To include who's coming and going from their compound."

"Point taken," Richardson said. "But this meeting with the SEPES officials," Richardson surmised. "I'm assuming he had classified documents with him. Or no?"

"He did," Koval said. "Several documents. In a locked attaché bag."

"We have them," the DCOS said assuredly with a wave of a hand. "The MPs picked the bag up at the scene and were sharp enough to bring it over to the Embassy. One of the Marines took custody."

"Good. That's one less thing to worry about," Richardson said. Frowning, he added, "I'm still concerned that we have a penetration here. At the Station? At NVOB? Both?"

"Hard to say," Koval replied. "I'm not claiming that NVOB is water-tight from a security point of view, but we aren't aware of any likely penetrations. Still, we'd be whistling past the graveyard if we thought that Saigon wasn't pigeon-holed with Communist sympathizers from top to bottom."

Richardson nodded agreeably. "Nonetheless, it would only be prudent that the CI unit keeps on with the internal investigation on NVOB and our local assets."

"Can't argue with that," Koval said truthfully. "If we can find them, let's root them out. The sooner, the better."

"And so, we will," Richardson said.

TWENTY-FOUR - UNREST

**January 1963
South Vietnam**

In early 1963 South Vietnam was beset by a raft of problems, some brought about by the international community and some of their own making. In addition to the strife of a growing insurgency, political feuding and post-colonial economics, a wave of religious unrest was beginning to sweep the country.

The majority of Vietnamese, eighty percent by some estimates, were practicing Buddhists. The ruling elites at the political level, however, were Roman Catholic. Not the least of the Catholic elite were the members of the Ngo family.

Buddhism was not a new concept. It emerged in the region of what is now India and Nepal in the Fifth Century BC. From India, it migrated to China, garnering acceptance and large numbers of adherents. And from China it flowed down into Vietnam, where its ceremonies and imagery coincided nicely with traditional Vietnamese beliefs and practices.

Catholicism, on the other hand, did not have such a well-defined historical track record with the people. It was not until the Sixteenth Century AD that the first European missionaries arrived in the country. Two hundred years later, the faith began to gain something of a modest foothold on the ground. Obviously, it was assisted in its efforts by the French colonization of Indochina in the latter years of the century.

By 1963 the most prominent Catholics in the country were Ngo Dinh Diem, the President, his brother Ngo Dinh Nhu and his sister-in-law Tran Le Xuan, better known to Westerners as Madame Nhu.

On May 8th, a large number of Buddhists demonstrated in the city of Hue. Their cause was Diem's recent ban on the display of religious flags. Police responded, eventually firing on the demonstrators, killing several of them. The Buddhist clergy appealed to the government for legal equality with Catholicism and punishment for the shooters.

Ambassador Nolting unsuccessfully attempted to pressure Diem to deal with the grievances and take responsibility for the actions of the 8th. Diem's rejection led to a protest of several hundred monks in front of the National Assembly in Saigon.

Earlier, Diem had been an up-and-coming politician who was appointed to be Prime Minister in 1954 under the Emperor, Bao Dai. Diem repaid the emperor by staging a much-criticized referendum in 1955. The referendum culminated in Diem declaring himself to be President of the newly formed Republic of South Vietnam.

The policies that Diem promoted were decidedly pro-Catholic. And at the expense of the Buddhist majority. This extended to the senior ranks of the military where the commanding officers were Catholic, or at least professed to be so, in order to further their career opportunities.

It was not to serve them well in the long term.

TWENTY-FIVE – STATION HOSPITAL

Saigon
February 11, 1963

Monday.

It was Laird's first workday back in Saigon after being released from the hospital. He still had a bandage over one eye. His face bore a number of red blotches from the burns and cuts that he had experienced in the attack.

After his discharge from the hospital, Laird was given the option of curtailing from the NVOB and returning to the US. Declining the offer, his developing relationship with Tuyet not being the least of reasons, he opted to take a two-week medical R&R in neighboring Singapore before returning to duty.

Tuyet was able to get away as well, joining him in Singapore for the second week of his medical leave. For a short while, they were almost able to get past the war and its turmoil. Almost.

That Monday morning, Laird was back at the medical facility, accompanied by Tuyet. They were in the building that the US Navy called *Station Hospital Saigon*, having taken it over from the Army medical staff some time earlier.

One of the orderlies escorted them up to XL's floor, down the sterile corridor and into his room. When they entered, they found the patient, Xiao Lin, pale and weak and still confined to his bed.

Contrary to earlier fears, XL had survived both the VC attack as well as subsequent multiple surgeries. Although the Navy doctors had saved his life, they could not restore his health. XL was to be invalided out of service with the Agency.

Seated next to his bed was a familiar figure, Jim Koval. In another chair was a less familiar personage, a wizened fellow who was introduced as XL's father.

Now that all had arrived, Koval rose to his feet and pulled an official-looking certificate from his briefcase. It was, he read, an award from the US Government, citing XL for his devotion to duty and recent bravery in the face of enemy action. It noted that he was to be placed on medical retirement with a suitable pension in recognition of his service.

As the senior Lin spoke no English, Tuyet translated for the Americans. She expressed their heartfelt appreciation for the loyalty and bravery shown by his son.

Rising from his chair, the senior Lin accepted the certificate respectfully. Bowing his head to Koval in recognition of his status, he uttered what appeared to be a prepared statement of his own.

"He says that he thanks you on behalf of his son and his family," Tuyet translated. "He said that he is very proud of his son and of his work with the American Government."

Koval took the senior Lin's hand in both of his and held it tightly. Then, nodding to the assemblage, he turned and left the room.

Laird shook the older man's hand as well. And then, giving XL's shoulder a squeeze in farewell, did the same.

TWENTY-SIX - VANN

Washington, DC
April 1963

In April, Lieutenant Colonel John Paul Vann's Vietnamese tour was finally over. The officer who had been the senior US advisor to the ARVN at the Battle of Ap Bac was heading back to the States. His new assignment would be in the Pentagon.

Vann's new stateside job involved financial oversight of the various Special Forces projects in Vietnam. Perhaps the bean-counting aspect of the assignment did not appeal to his basic nature. In any event, he became engaged in numerous interviews of returning officers, intent upon preparing a report on their joint experiences in-country.

His findings were troubling. He claimed that the combat body count figures, upon which the US was increasingly focused, were being inflated by a factor of two-thirds. Unfortunately, the dead frequently included innocent civilians who had been caught up in the violence.

Moreover, Vann argued, the widespread civilian deaths among the Vietnamese populace were being caused by the indiscriminate use, primarily on behalf of our ARVN allies, of air strikes and long-distance artillery fires. These practices, he said, were alienating the populace and driving them further into the arms of the VC.

Impressed by his findings, Vann was invited to brief the general officers of the Joint Chiefs of Staff (JCS). When the Chairman of the JCS learned of the essence of his report, and more significantly, of its conflict with information coming in from MACV commander General Paul Harkens, the briefing was abruptly cancelled.

At that point, Vann did not need to be a psychic to see that his military career, which began as a private in the Army Air Corps in 1943 and had peaked as a field grade officer, was effectively over. He retired from the Army that same July.

However, Vann was not finished with Vietnam, nor it with him.

Vann later returned to the country in 1965 as a civilian government official. He eventually served as a senior province advisor with the US Agency for International Development, or

Black Entry

USAID. In that capacity, he had the unusual position of a civilian supervising certain military operations.

In an ironic tragedy, that is where he was to meet his death. In June of 1972, at the age of 47, Vann was killed in a helicopter crash near Kon Tum.

He is buried in Arlington National Cemetery.

TWENTY-SEVEN – JASON

North Vietnam
May 14, 1963

The members of the JASON team were tense and silent. They were sitting in the bay of the transport that was flying them north, just off the enemy coast. On the floor between them were the bundles of supplies that were to be dropped in along with them.

Time-wise, they were following the four-man PEGASUS team, which had been inserted in April.

NVOB was keenly hoping for a success that night. Two earlier attempts had been canceled. One drop, that of the EUROPA team, was called off due to bad weather conditions. Another, with supplies destined for Team PEGASUS, ended in failure when the parachute straps of the bundles broke away after being kicked out of the plane.

Equipment failures were the least of the Station's concerns. Weeks earlier, the Chinese government had announced that it would militarily come to the aid of North Vietnam, if it were attacked by the United States. More recently, a Chinese spokesman stated that it was prepared to form a strategic rear area for the North Vietnamese. The threat of an expanding war was ominous.

Such political concerns occupied exactly no space in the minds of those on the aircraft that night.

At the appointed time, the aircraft turned westward, crossing over the coast of North Vietnam. The Jumpmaster pulled open the door as a red light came on above it. The team could feel the rush of cool air now blowing in through the doorway.

Minutes later, the Jumpmaster made an upward gesture with both arms. The JASON team members pushed themselves upright and, weighted down by their parachutes and personal gear, waddled the few feet toward the open doorway in the rear of the aircraft.

There they waited, eyes on the glowing red light.

After what seemed to be an interminable amount of time, a bell rang throughout the cabin, and the red light went off – replaced by a green one.

The Jumpmaster shoved their bundles out the door. The team members quickly followed, leaping out into the unknowable dark sky over North Vietnam.

The Jumpmaster paused, briefly peering out at them, and then pulled the door closed. The pilot turned the nose of the aircraft to the east and headed back for the coast. And then to the safety of South Vietnamese territory.

* * *

The aircrew later reported that Team JASON had been successfully dropped at the appointed coordinates. They went on to say that they observed that all of the member's parachutes had successfully deployed, ensuring a safe landing.

Subsequent reporting showed that JASON never came up on the air. That is to say that they never successfully activated their radio.

They were gone.

TWENTY-EIGHT - SACRED SWORD

Saigon
May 23, 1963

Jim Koval and Paul Sarpi were the two NVOB staffers called over to the Station that morning to sit in on the briefing.

An unfamiliar figure waited expectantly at the front of the room with a plastic clicker in his hand. A blank screen was set up behind him against the wall. A Kodak cassette slide player hummed along expectantly on the table in front of him.

"Know this guy?" Sarpi asked, jostling a styrofoam cup of coffee as they settled into their seats.

"Not really, no," Koval said. "He came in from Headquarters a month or so ago. Worked in Political Action, as far as I know."

"Actually, Psychological Operations," another Agency staffer seated nearby provided. "They say Colby latched onto him at Langley. Liked what he saw, and sent him out here."

"Colby?" Koval echoed.

The other staffer nodded. "Word is that he's a born-again PsyOps guy now."

The group nodded respectfully as COS Richardson came in and acknowledged the attendees with a wave of the hand.

"Everyone, thanks for coming in," Richardson said as the room quieted down. "While what you're about to hear may not necessarily involve all of you, I think it's worthwhile for each of your sections to be apprised of this upcoming operation."

The COS took a seat in the front row. "Okay Herb," he said, crossing his legs. "The floor is yours. Take it away."

"Yes sir," the stranger said, centering himself in front of the screen.

"Good morning all," he began. "As some of you know, my name is Herb. And, as they say, I'm from Washington, and I'm here to help."

The quip drew the expected rattle of snickers from the assembled group.

"Anyhow," he continued, "the Chief asked me to keep this short since this is a busy Station and we all have a lot to do. So, without any further ado..."

He squeezed the clicker and a slide reading *Sacred Sword of the Patriots League* popped onto the screen.

"The purpose of this brief is to give you all a brief overview of a new PsyOps project that we are gearing up. This is aimed at weakening the infrastructure of the North and give them a little extra something to think about. Needless to say, this briefing is classified at the Top Secret level in its entirety."

The next slide was that of a large green tortoise. "You may believe it or not, but the story centers about the appearance of a Golden Turtle God."

Sarpi nudged Koval in the ribs. "They told me that this would be an interesting career," he jibbed lowly.

Koval was unmoved.

"But first, some local and regional history," Herb continued. The next slide was that of a map of Vietnam and China.

"China and Vietnam have always had a contentious relationship. Neighbors and all that." He squeezed the clicker again.

"*Zhong Guo*, the Middle Kingdom," Herb said as an expanded map of China flashed onto the screen.

"From the thirteenth to the fourteenth centuries AD, the Mongols ruled the area that we now think of as China... To put this in some historical context, during the fourteenth century, neighboring Japan was then in its feudal period with warring samurai families battling each other. In fact, they were less than a hundred years past surviving their own failed invasion attempt from the Mongols. The Japanese attributed their defeat of the Mongols to a typhoon that they called the *Divine Wind*, or the *Kamikaze*."

A color photo of a globe appeared.

"It was the medieval age in Europe," he continued. "The enthusiasm of the Crusades had largely expired. The Black Plague, in some instances, was killing off half of the populations across the continent. The Renaissance was only beginning to take shape in Italy.

"The last of the Crusader strongpoints were expelled in the Mideast, which was also dealing with the effects of the Plague. The Ottomans captured Constantinople, the former capital of the Eastern Roman Empire. Islam was spreading in Africa.

"Finally, in the Americas, the indigenous peoples still held sway, both north and south. The various tribal communities in the north;

Incas, Aztecs and Mayas in the south. The first of the European settlers were more than three centuries from arrival."

Herb glanced over his audience to ensure that he still had their attention. "So much for the Mongols... In 1368 the Ming Dynasty drove them out of power. Not surprisingly, the Mings then eventually looked about thinking in terms of expansion. What they saw, to their south, was Vietnam."

The next slide was a map of North Vietnam. "In 1406, or thereabouts, the Ming decided to invade Vietnam. They did so with more than 200,000 soldiers and, within a year, they were in control."

An artist's depiction of a throng of armored, helmeted and spear-carrying Chinese warriors appeared on the screen.

"Unfortunately, the Mings proved to be pretty harsh rulers," Herb said. "So, it didn't take long for a Vietnamese resistance force to emerge."

Another rachet of the slide carousel produced the artistic drawing of a large sword with a long, slightly curved blade.

"As it developed, an aristocratic landowner from *Thanh Hoa* province, just south of Hanoi, appeared to take charge of the resistance. His name was Le Loi.

"Le Loi himself had a good sense of medieval era PsyOps," Herb explained. "It is said that he doctored the leaves of the forest trees with a thin paste. The tracings of the paste read that he, Le Loi, was the *true king* of Vietnam. After the forest ants chewed away the paste, the people read the perforated messages on the leaves and proclaimed him to be their leader... Pretty damn clever."

Herb took a sip of water and continued his lecture. "According to the legend, a god in the form of a golden turtle appeared from a lake and presented Le with a magical sword. The blade was engraved with the words: *By the Will of Heaven*. This was the very sword that Le used to lead his people against the Chinese."

The slide show reverted to a map of North Vietnam.

"Finding the Mings to be too powerful, Le adopted a guerrilla strategy. His forces fell back to strongholds in the largely coastal *Ha Tinh* mountains. From there, for the next two decades, they conducted an unrelenting series of ambushes and costly surprise attacks against the Ming troops.

A slide of coastal northern Vietnam appeared.

"By 1428, the Mings had suffered enough punishment. They pulled out of Vietnam, and Le was proclaimed to be king. His dynasty lasted for another three hundred years. Even now, the North Vietnamese hold Le Loi as a national hero. Second only in prestige to that of Uncle Ho himself."

"And the turtle..." Richardson prompted.

"Yes, of course," Herb said. "According to the story, after peace had prevailed, Le Loi was one day enjoying a cruise on a small lake in the middle of Hanoi. Just then, a giant turtle suddenly emerged from the water. Startled, Le Loi drew the magic sword to defend himself. The turtle, however, was quicker. It seized the sword with its mouth and dove back into the depths of the lake.

"Enraged, Le Loi had the lake drained. But there was no sign of either the turtle. Nor of his famous sword...

"After he calmed down for a bit, it occurred to him that he had only been given the sword as a mandate of heaven to defeat the Ming invaders. That task accomplished, the sword was taken back by the god for safekeeping until it would be needed once again.

"Le Loi then renamed the lake as *Ho Hoan Kiem*, or the *Lake of the Returned Sword,* as it is still called today. The local populace knows this story well."

Jim Koval stirred in his seat. "All very interesting," he said. "But how does this apply to our operations in the North?"

The briefer was ready for him.

"We're going to bring the tale of Le Loi up to date," he replied. "Our PsyOps plan involves the formation of a fictional national resistance movement in the North that, as noted, we are calling the *Sacred Sword of the Patriots League.* As we envision it, the program will consist of two primary themes: that of emphasizing traditional Vietnamese nationalism and that of fostering resentment of the corrupt leadership in Hanoi."

A black and white photograph of struggling Vietnamese peasants came onto the screen.

"As most of you may know, in 1953, following the Chinese model, North Vietnam instituted an aggressive land reform campaign. It was a violent exercise in the class struggle. Very painful and disruptive in the countryside. Thousands of landlords were either executed or imprisoned. And it was a disaster. The populace *hated* it.

"The land reform policy led to an actual revolt. It took place in 1956 in the *Quynh Luu* district, a traditionally Catholic area. Ho Chi Minh's home province, I might add. The resultant action by the government reportedly killed or otherwise disposed of 6,000 of the protestors.

"The seeds of resentment are still there, I'm happy to say. So, that will be the basis of our corruption theme: the Communist leaders are doing very well; the peasantry is suffering. Rise up and oppose the regime."

The original SSPL slide came back up on the screen.

"Along with the corruption theme, we will be talking about the supposedly disenchanted members of the Viet Minh. These are the combat veterans who fought the French on behalf of their homeland. According to *our* version of history, these are the disillusioned patriots who battled the foreigners. They resent the current overlords and see a growing tendency of the Chinese to resume their influence in the country. It is they, the old Viet Minh veterans, who form the basis of the notional SSPL with the goal of overthrowing the Hanoi regime. They will be presented as nationalists who want to rid the country of all foreign interests. Especially the Chinese."

"And that would also apply to us," someone added.

"And us," Herb agreed. "That's the theme."

The room was briefly silent as they digested the information.

At last, Sarpi raised a hand tentatively to catch Herb's attention. "Yes?"

"Uh, Herb... Approximately how many giant turtles do you plan to recruit for this operation?"

Herb's face reddened slightly as several in the audience chuckled, but he rolled on with it. "No money in the budget for turtles, I'm afraid," he said. "SSPL will be focusing on black radio broadcasts, pamphlets, leafleting and deception operations via agents of influence on the ground... *Propaganda of the deed*, as our friends in the Viet Cong like to say.

"The central idea is to cause enough concern in Hanoi to the extent that they are obliged to divert forces from the war effort to deal with problems in their own back yard. To their cost."

"Okay," COS Richardson said, rising to his feet. "I think that's about all the time we've allotted for today's brief. There will be more on this in the future, to include assignments to the various sections to assist. But for now, I'm going to let you comedians get back to your day jobs. Off you go."

TWENTY-NINE - LYRE

NVOB - Saigon
May 29, 1963

Tate sat alone in his office. Outside, darkness had fallen. As it was after hours, he felt justified in nursing a beer while going through his paperwork. Or several.

He was reading an update on LYRE, a team he had taken over after returning from his sick leave. As was all too often the case, the news was not good.

Team LYRE was a sabotage unit consisting of seven personnel. Unlike the usual air drop insertions, this one was a maritime operation.

On December 30th of 1962, the team was delivered to the North via a sea-going junk. All of the routine precautions had been followed. The team was comprised of were seven well-trained men who were dedicated to the cause. They made landfall, as scheduled, in an uninhabited coastal area called *Deo Ngang*. The landing was a success. Unopposed.

Once again however, the team quickly went silent. And they remained quiet for the following five months, never having made radio contact with NVOB.

That May morning, NVOB and the Station were updated on the status of LYRE, courtesy of Radio Hanoi.

The North Vietnamese announced that LYRE was no more. They announced that five of the team members were immediately captured upon landing. The remaining two escaped but were apprehended a few days later.

Tate swore softly and opened another beer.

THIRTY - THE MONK

Saigon, South Vietnam
June 11, 1963

The day was hot and humid in Saigon; but how was that different than most other days in-country?

Jim Koval had stationed himself at one of the city's major intersections near the Cambodian Embassy. Along with him was one of the Station's junior officers, also sent along to observe and report. It was no secret that a significant socio-political development was about to happen. Just what that might be, they weren't quite sure.

Eight days earlier, there had been a confrontation between government troops and Buddhist protestors in the ancient city of Hue, almost six hundred miles to the north.

In 1960 Diem's older brother had been appointed to be the Catholic archbishop of the city. Despite of – or maybe because of – the fact that Hue had been the religious center of Vietnam for a thousand years, the appointment was not well received in all circles.

On June 3rd, some fifteen hundred Buddhist protestors in Hue attempted to cross a bridge over the Perfume River. Their goal was a historic pagoda called the *Tu Dam*. Massed troops of the ARVN stood in their way.

The demonstrators were primarily composed of students, both of high school and college age. When their progress was stopped by the military, they planted themselves on the ground and stolidly refused to leave.

After several hours of noisy confrontation, the ARVN troops deployed what they later claimed to be tear gas on the crowd. The troops eventually succeeded in dispersing the masses, with many of them ending up in hospitals for chemical injuries. Several had reportedly been killed in the melee following the gassing.

Given the number of patients who had suffered a variety of burns to the skin, the Buddhists claimed it was not tear gas, but a form of poison gas that had been employed against them.

Later studies determined that the chemical was likely not poison gas as alleged, but rather an outdated French Army chemical that, in some cases, dated as far back as World War I.

Bad enough, Koval knew. But the worse was to come in the in the capital itself. He did not have long to wait.

From down the street came an orderly procession of orange-robed Buddhist monks. They were followed and surrounded by a noisy throng of fellow believers. At their head was a solemn gaunt monk whose name, Koval was later to learn, was Thich Quang Duc.

Public security forces were on hand but were clearly apprehensive of stepping in, for fear of inciting the crowd. They were far outnumbered by onlookers and members of the national and foreign press, all of whom had gotten wind of a developing story.

The protestors stopped just short of the intersection. They grew quieter, some openly in tears, as Quang Duc turned to address them briefly.

As Koval and the junior officer watched apprehensively, Quang Duc finished his address and stepped away from the assemblage of his fellows. Unceremoniously, he dropped into a cross-legged sitting position of meditation right there in the street.

Accompanied by the chanting of the monks and the increasing murmurs of the crowd, a fellow monk stepped up behind him with what appeared to Koval to be a large plastic fuel container.

All doubts as to the intent of the demonstration vanished when the second monk uncapped the container and began to pour five gallons of gasoline over Quang Duc's head and shoulders.

Quang Duc appeared to be the very essence of calm. Seemingly unaware of the turmoil developing around him, he began to chant in low rhythmic tones as he fingered a set of prayer beads that hung about his neck. This continued along for several more minutes as all sides watched uneasily.

And then there was a furtive movement, almost imperceptively, with the thin fingers of the chanting monk.

Koval looked on in disbelief as Quang Duc produced a wooden match. Pausing momentarily, he somehow struck the match alight and dropped it onto the gasoline-soaked robes in his lap.

Flames immediately enveloped the monk with a rush of air. The crowd cried out loudly and wailed in response. Quang Duc nevertheless continued to sit stock still, awash in the liquid flares of the conflagration.

A city fire truck attempted to approach the scene, but the bodies of the protestors blocked it. Unencumbered, the form of Quang Duc continued to burn for several more minutes until it toppled over to the ground.

A fellow monk then appeared with a fire extinguisher to douse the flames. Successful, they placed the body into a wooden casket. An estimated one thousand supporters followed the casket as it was transported to their pagoda, where it was finally cremated.

As another observer, David Halberstam of the New York Times, was later to write: *"Flames were coming from a human being; his body was slowly withering and shriveling up, his head blackening and charring. In the air was the smell of burning human flesh; human beings burn surprisingly quickly. Behind me I could hear the sobbing of the Vietnamese who were now gathering. I was too shocked to cry, too confused to take notes or ask questions, too bewildered to even think... As he burned, he never moved a muscle, never uttered a sound..."*

Koval and the junior officer took their leave, hustling back to the Embassy. There would, Koval knew, be significant implications of this day's deed.

THIRTY-ONE - DRAGON LADY

Saigon, South Vietnam
June 1963

She had been born in Hanoi to wealthy, Catholic parents. Her given name was Tran Le Xuan, but she was better known as *Madame Nhu*, given her marriage to the President's brother. As the President, Ngo Dinh Diem, was a bachelor, she was considered to be the de facto First Lady of Vietnam.

With regard to her striking looks and Machiavellian personality, she was also frequently referred to in the press as *The Dragon Lady*. It was a nickname that she did not discourage.

Le Xuan was a mixed blessing to the political interests of the Ngo family. She was an ardent supporter of their conservative policies and a vocal critic of their opponents. During Diem's 1955 referendum that sidelined Emperor Bao Dai, she recommended to Diem that he take advantage of the situation to *crush* all of his political opponents. He followed her advice, and she briefly gained a seat in the National Assembly.

Le Xuan's blunt outspokenness was particularly apparent when it came to the Buddhists. And her comments were increasingly drawing criticism, both at home and abroad.

Her response to the self-immolation of the monk - Quang Duc - was hardly sympathetic.

"I may shock some by saying that I would beat such provocateurs ten times more if they wore monks' robes," she said.

With a view toward the recent demise of Quang Duc, she said that she would "... clap hands at seeing another monk barbecue show, for one cannot be responsible for the madness of others." She added that she would provide mustard as a condiment for the next such exhibition.

Her comments invited international criticism of the Saigon establishment. Such criticism even included that of her father.

Le Xuan would later refer to the Buddhists as seditionists who used Communist tactics to subvert Vietnam.

A later historian would later comment that she had put the *finishing touch* on the Diem regime.

THIRTY-TWO - GONE ASTRAY

Saigon, South Vietnam
July 1963

By July, NVOB had learned that Team PEGASUS was lost.

PEGASUS, which had been inserted in April, failed to make radio contact with NVOB for two weeks. When they did, they reported having had problems with the tight drop zone and subsequent difficulties in regrouping once on the ground.

Still, NVOB knew that delays in initial contact from personnel newly arrived in the North were not uncommon.

And now, Hanoi announced that the men of PEGASUS had all been captured, tried and imprisoned for their crimes. But at least they were ostensibly still alive.

The month of July began with the good news of improved logical capacity. Until then, the primary aircraft used for ferrying agent teams north and making re-supply runs was the Douglas DC-4. The venerable DC-4's of World War II vintage, were being replaced by the newer Fairchild C-123's. Five of them had arrived in-country and were placed at the disposal of the station – and NVOB.

On July 2nd the first C-123 mission went north, carrying Team GIANT. The aircrew dropped them into the mountains that lay west of the city of Vinh. Although the drop was judged a success, GIANT never came up on the air to make contact with Saigon. Their status was unknown.

On the 4th, a decision was made to send one of the DC-4 fleet on a final operation. The plane carried Team PACKER, a sabotage element whose target was the same stretch of railway that an earlier team – BELL - had attempted to destroy. The track ran on a stretch that was seventy-five kilometers north of Hanoi and went into China.

The aircrew of the DC-4 that dropped PACKER communicated back that all of the parachutes had opened and that the members appeared to have landed successfully. The aircraft then turned and headed for a further point to drop supplies to yet another team.

The DC-4 never returned home.

Having no evidence of enemy ground fire, the Station assumed that the pilot of the low-flying plane misjudged the terrain and crashed against the side of a mountain in the darkness.

Despite the multiple operational setbacks, someone in the Station had the confidence to include the following observation in a cable to CIA Headquarters:

"Careful planning and professional airmanship can eliminate virtually all danger."

THIRTY-THREE - SOG

July 1963
Washington, DC

NVOB, the North Vietnam Operational Branch, became active in 1961 as *Project Tiger*, a CIA operation designed to infiltrate the North under the direction of Saigon Chief of Station Bill Colby.

In July of 1963, the senior levels of the Central Intelligence Agency and the Department of Defense reached an agreement that such operations would transfer from CIA to Defense management, effective as of January 1964.

The new organization in charge of the penetration of North Vietnam was to be called *MACV-SOG*, or the Military Assistance Command, Vietnam – Studies and Observations Group.

The *SOG* tag was designed to be an academic-sounding cover, thin though it might be, for what would be a lethal Special Forces unit. Over the next several years, that unit would establish a heroic record of almost suicidal cross border forays into Laos, Cambodia and North Vietnam, with the aim of conducting reconnaissance, communications interception and prisoner snatching missions.

Koval and his crew were now officially placed on a five- month countdown.

THIRTY-FOUR - EASY

North Vietnam
August 11, 1963

Team EASY jumped into North Vietnam on the 11th of August. The selected drop site was near the Laotian border. As a mark of honor, EASY was designated to be the first of the SSPL propaganda units.

Along with spreading leaflets and popularizing the story of the League among the citizenry, they also had the mission of collecting intelligence and committing acts of sabotage.

EASY landed successfully and soon came up on the air to confirm their positive status with Saigon.

Several weeks later another SSPL team, this one called SWAN, went into the Cao Bang area in northernmost Vietnam. They were captured upon landing.

In later years, the Agency concluded that EASY, which had been viewed by NVOB as one of their greater successes, had been almost immediately compromised upon arrival.

* * *

In Langley that month, Bill Colby, Director of the Far East Division met with Deputy Director of Plans, or the DDP. At the time, the DDP was the head of the Clandestine Services in what was to be later called the Directorate of Operations.

In his meeting, Colby told the DDP that, in his estimation, "... no intelligence of value has been, or is likely to be, obtained from such operations... to include sabotage operations."

He recommended that the focus should be on the areas of political and psychological operations.

However, he didn't say how that would be accomplished.

THIRTY-FIVE - XA LOI

August 21, 1963
Saigon, South Vietnam

Shortly after midnight on August 21st, a series of violent raids were conducted on Buddhist pagodas across South Vietnam, but especially in the cities of Hue and Saigon. The raids were under the command of Colonel Le Quang Tung, an officer of the ARVN Special Forces.

And Le Quang Tung reported to Ngo Dinh Nhu, who supervised a number of the various security services on behalf of his presidential brother, Ngo Dinh Diem.

The declared reason for the raids was to suppress the increasing numbers of Buddhist protest demonstrations against the government. The two most significant raids were those against the Tu Dam pagoda in Hue and that against the Xa Loi pagoda in Saigon.

After the employment of heavily armed forces, including battering rams and explosives, an estimated hundreds of people were killed. Some 1,400 had been arrested.

The result was a political and public relations disaster for the Diem regime – and their American supporters.

THIRTY-SIX - AMBO

August 26, 1963
Saigon, South Vietnam

Frederick Nolting had been the US Ambassador to South Vietnam since May of 1961. By the summer of 1963, JFK's advisors were of the opinion that Nolting, a career Foreign Service Officer, had *gone native* insofar as the Diem regime was concerned. It was a criticism that was often directed to Foreign Service personnel. It implied that the officer concerned had begun to identify too closely with the interests of the local government officials at the expense of furthering US policies. Sometimes the charge was justified; other times, not.

In particular, Nolting was thought to be unnecessarily sympathetic to Diems's brother Nhu. Madame Nhu's husband was believed to be the true power behind the throne in Saigon.

In subsequent weeks, Nolting would claim that Nhu had no role in the infamous pagoda raids and that Diem was a *man of integrity* who made good on his promises to the United States, or had at least made every effort to have done so.

Chief of Station Richardson disagreed. Based on a meeting he had with Nhu in mid-July, he saw the excitable Nhu as being obsessed with his belief that the Buddhists were not only spreading Communist propaganda but were actively concealing Communist agents in their pagodas.

Nhu went so far as to tell Richardson that he had taken to meeting regularly with senior ARVN generals. In the course of those meetings, he said that he discussed the possibility of a coup against his brother. The goal, he said - truthfully or not - was to elicit guilty comments from the generals themselves.

By August, JFK had decided to replace Nolting with a Republican from Massachusetts, Henry Cabot Lodge. As a former senator, and having been previously appointed by President Eisenhower as the Ambassador to the United Nations, Lodge was seen a steady choice to manage the unraveling situation.

And so, it was done.

Having replaced Nolting, Lodge formally presented his ambassadorial credentials to President Diem on August 26th.

After offering an unsolicited brief lesson on the value of public relations in politics, Lodge was treated to a two-hour lecture from Diem on the importance of the Ngo family and the problems of South Vietnam as an underdeveloped country.

On August 24th Lodge received an *IMMEDIATE* cable, that being the second-highest level of cable precedence, from the State Department in Washington. In what came to be called the Hillsman Telegram, the Top-Secret message charged Lodge to pressure Diem to remove his brother. The lines of its second paragraph were unambiguous:

"*The US Government cannot tolerate the situation in which power lies in Nhu's hands,*" it read. "*Diem must be given the chance to rid himself of Nhu and his coterie and replace them with the best military and political personalities available.*"

The cable continued, "*We wish (to) give Diem reasonable opportunity to remove Nhu, but if he remains obdurate, then we are prepared to accept the obvious implication that we can no longer support Diem. You may also tell appropriate military commanders that we will give them direct support in any interim period of breakdown of central government mechanism.*"

After urging Lodge to examine possibilities for a replacement of Diem, it reminded him that "*... we will back you to the hilt on actions you take to achieve our objectives.*"

A later historian would describe the Hillsman Telegram as "the single most controversial cable of the Vietnam War."

THIRTY-SEVEN - GO CONG

Saigon, South Vietnam
September 5, 1963

Jay Laird was having lunch in the small cafeteria at NVOB when Sarpi dropped into a chair on the other side of the table. Unwrapping a sandwich, Sarpi noticed that Laird was still absently fingering the scar that stood out prominently above his eyebrow. It was a habit that he had acquired since the VC ambush downtown, months ago.

"A war souvenir," Laird grumped, scanning a newspaper that was folded next to his plate.

"Doesn't look so bad," Sarpi said. "Lucky you still have a head there to put the scar on."

"I guess... Maybe you should try one."

"I'll look into it," Sarpi nodded to the newspaper, chewing. "What's got your attention there?"

"JFK," Laird answered. "He was interviewed by Cronkite on CBS the other day... The subject of Vietnam came up, of course."

"And?"

Laird lifted the paper up for a better view. "He told Uncle Walter that he didn't think the war here can be won without a greater effort by the Saigon government... We can help, he said, but they are the ones who will either win it or lose it."

"No shit," Sarpi commented. "Where'd he ever get that idea?"

Laird looked at his partner over the paper and continued. "He said that he thinks the government here has lost touch with the people. Cites the Buddhist issue. Says that it can still win but may need a change in its policies. Or a change in its personnel."

Sarpi grunted.

"But still," Laird added. "Kennedy thinks that for us to bail out of here would be a *'great mistake.'*"

"Changes in personnel," Sarpi repeated. "And so there may be. What's your source over at SEPES make of the local political situation?"

Laird frowned. "Source? You mean Tuyet? She's not my *source* over there."

Sarpi shook his head. "Really? You're the one sleeping with her. Either she's your source, or you're her's, buddy."

Miffed, Laird considered giving his partner and sponsor the middle finger but relented.

And then he relented again and gave him the finger.

"Well," Sarpi said, finishing the sandwich and reaching for a bottle of Coca-Cola. "So much for that... But there is a little bit of good news from down in the Delta."

"That battle this week..." Laird began.

"To call it a battle might be a little much of a description," Sarpi interrupted. "But there was an attack on US and ARVN forces near the town of Go Cong. From what I'm reading, it seems that the VC honchos were looking to pull off a second Ap Bac type of victory down there.

"Not insignificantly, he added, "there is a historical context."

"Like what?"

"Back around 1862, a Viet resistance leader named Truong Dinh staged a surprise attack on a French colonial fortress at Go Cong. That one was a success. Even the French later said that the Vietnamese seemed to be driven by a spirit of national independence."

"But our Go Cong?"

"Not so good for the other team," Sarpi said. "A combination of artillery and sniper fire by US troops and the ARVNs cut them short. The VC lost around a hundred and fifty, dead or captured."

"Good," Laird observed. "*Sat Cong.*"

Sarpi raised his Coke bottle in a toast. "*Sat Cong,*" he agreed.

THIRTY-EIGHT - FACT FINDING

September 10, 1963
Washington, DC

Marine Corps Major General Victor Krulak and senior Foreign Service Officer Joseph Mendenhall were in the White House for a meeting with President Kennedy.

Krulak was the Special Assistant for Counterinsurgency and Special Activities for the Joint Chiefs, while Mendenhall was a State Department specialist on Vietnamese affairs. Both had just returned from a four-day fact-finding trip to South Vietnam.

They had visited a country that was awash with civil unrest in the wake of the pagoda raids and killings of Buddhists. The US National Security Council had also just met in view of the worsening relations between Washington and Saigon.

Focusing on their respective areas of expertise, the two men split up while in country. Krulak visited military leaders in ten different locations. He followed that up with interviews of both Ambassador Lodge and the commander of US forces, General Harkins.

For his part, Mendenhall toured Da Nang, Hue and Saigon, among others, meeting primarily with Vietnamese political figures.

In his upbeat report, Krulak told the President that the ARVN was generally making good progress against the VC. Further, it was his belief that the average Vietnamese soldier and his officers would not be affected by the widespread unhappiness with Diem and his people.

On the contrary, it was Mendenhall's view that the city dwellers were largely in opposition to Diem. The future, he said, might include a religious civil war. He added that many members of the populace were coming to suspect that life might actually be better under the Communists.

Somewhat taken aback by the two conflicting reports, Kennedy was moved to ask his advisors if they had, in fact, both been to the same country.

THIRTY-NINE - BIG MINH

Saigon, South Vietnam
October 1963

In 1963, Lucien Conein was sent to Saigon as part of the CIA Station. Officially, however, he was assigned to be an advisor to the South Vietnamese Ministry of the Interior.

A colorful character, Conein had been born in Paris, France, but his parents sent him to live with an aunt in the state of Kansas. When World War II broke out, he hurried to join the French Army. Following their surrender to the Germans a year later, he just as quickly deserted.

Later spotted by the American OSS, Conein was recruited and parachuted back into France to lead local resistance units. There, he worked actively with both American OSS teams and British SOE units.

When the war in Europe ended, Conein relocated to French Indochina to lead teams against the occupying Japanese. And now, decades later, he was back in the region.

One of Conein's primary local contacts was an ARVN general named Duong Van Minh. Weighing in at some 200 pounds and a height of six feet, unusual dimensions for a Vietnamese, he was nicknamed *Big Minh*.

Conein had earlier been pinged by another ARVN general during the Embassy's 4th of July celebrations. The two knew each other from their WW II days. The general floated the suggestion that it would be good to know what the position of the US Embassy would be in the event of an anti-Diem coup. Conein duly reported the contact back to Washington.

In October, Conein met with Big Minh. As was the case with the July contact, Minh inquired about the position of the US Government insofar as support of Diem was concerned.

The situation, said Minh, was deteriorating. He stated that there was a need to change the national leadership or face losing the struggle to the Viet Cong. He added that he was hardly the only ARVN general who held such a view.

According to Minh, there were only three possible outcomes to the situation:

- The easiest option - the assassination of Nhu, with the retention of Diem in power
- The encirclement of Saigon by ARVN units, as a show of strength
- Direct confrontation between coup and loyalist ARVN units within Saigon itself

Later in the month, another ARVN general told Conein that October 26th had been set as the date of the planned coup.

When General Harkins learned of this, he passed back the message that the United States was opposed to the concept of a coup, but that it would not take any action to thwart a change in government.

The follow-on message was that the United States would not deny economic or military support to a new government, providing that it appeared to be capable of an increased level of military effectiveness against the Communist enemy.

FORTY - JOCKO

Washington, DC
October 1963

Early in October, Chief of Station Jocko Richardson was recalled from Saigon and sent back to Washington. The official reason given for the recall was the time-tested, all-purpose excuse of *consultations*. Many in the know, however, doubted that he would ever return to post.

In truth, Richardson was not a favorite of Ambassador Lodge. The Chief of Mission tended to agree with certain dissident Vietnamese elements who believed that Richardson was becoming far too closely associated with Diem's brother, Nhu.

According to reports, Lodge conveyed the request to Washington that Richardson be removed and replaced with someone who would focus on intelligence collection and analysis – not politics. His concerns were carried to President Kennedy by no less a figure than Secretary of Defense McNamara.

CIA Director John McCone did not stand in the way of a requested replacement.

FORTY-ONE - COUP

November 1, 1963
Saigon

It was evening by the time that Jim Koval reached the NVOB offices. He had been out of the capital when the action kicked off earlier in the day. Tate and Laird were among the first of his officers that he encountered. He found the pair in the conference room, shuffling documents at a long, wooden table.

Laird and the others had been called into the NVOB offices throughout the afternoon and into the night. They had that duty in common with the members of the Station and, indeed, the entire staff of the Embassy. The air of Saigon rattled with the noise of gunfire as they traversed the streets.

"Update me," Koval said, dropping his day pack and a gunbelt onto the table. "The city's going batshit out there!"

"It's the coup," Tate said, absently chewing on the stub of an unlit cigar as he perused a document. "The one they've been rumoring about for the past few weeks."

"*The* coup?" Koval repeated. He had been otherwise consumed with attempts to salvage operations in the North.

"Looks like the generals have had enough with Diem," Laird said.

"Or enough of Brother Nhu," Tate chimed in. "Just as likely."

Koval pulled a bottle of beer from a small refrigerator and pushed the door closed with a knee. "If that's what it is, then the rumored killing of Diem's naval commander earlier may have been the kick-off event."

"Correct," Tate said. "He was shot and killed while driving along the Bien Hoa Highway today. Just before noon."

"About the same time that rebel troops under General Tran Van Don occupied the main police station, radio station and post office," Laird said, taking up the narrative. "And then Tran himself had a group of senior Viet generals arrested while they were having lunch at their O Club... That was when he formally announced the coup."

Koval took a swallow of beer. "And Diem is where right now?"

Black Entry

"Holed up inside the Gia Long Palace with his brother." It was Sarpi, coming into the conference room with a sheaf of the latest reports.

As Koval well knew, the Gia Long facility housed the interim offices of the President. Diem had relocated there after his permanent offices were damaged during the bombing by rebel Air Force pilots the year before. It was not a portent of good things to come.

"What's it looking like? Outcomes-wise."

Sarpi took a seat at the table. "Not good for Diem. His main protective assets, the ARVN Special Forces and the Presidential Guard are weakening. He's been sending out calls for loyal units to come to the capital at speed to save the regime. But..."

"But what?"

"Doesn't look like he's getting any takers."

* * *

The siege continued overnight. Diem set out his last message at 0400, Saturday morning. He was again calling for the loyalist units of the military to come and *"liberate the capital."*

At about the same time, Diem contacted Ambassador Lodge. The latter assured Diem that he would do all in his power to safeguard Diem and his family.

Two hours later, the rebel forces stormed the Gia Long Palace and took control of it.

Diem and Nhu, however, were not to be found. By means of an underground tunnel, the brothers had escaped the compound, making their way to an awaiting vehicle. From there, they were transported to the French church of St. Francis Xavier in the ethnic Chinese district of Cholon.

In Cholon, and sensing the inevitable, Diem entered into communication with the leaders of the rebel forces. Bowing to what appeared to be an inescapable reality, Diem agreed to surrender the presidency. With that came a guarantee that he and his family would be granted safe conduct out of Vietnam and into exile at a foreign locale.

According to the agreement, an APC, an M-113 armored personnel carrier, was sent to collect the two brothers. They were then to be transported to the ARVN headquarters, where arrangements for their disposition would be finalized.

Somewhere between Cholon and the military headquarters, a rebel ARVN captain gave the order - and both Ngo Dinh Diem and Ngo Dinh Nhu were shot and killed in the back of the APC.

The coup had succeeded.

General Big Minh was now in control of the government.

***

On November 2nd, as it did every day, the CIA delivered a Top-Secret document called *The President's Intelligence Checklist* to JFK. Among the items briefed were the following comments:

"1. South Vietnam

- a. The deaths of Diem and Nhu just about wrap up the generals' coup.
- b. Not all versions of the story are the same, but it would appear that the brothers either committed suicide or they were done in after surrendering. We suspect the latter."

FORTY-TWO - SUMMIT

Camp Smith
Honolulu, Hawaii
November 21, 1963

By late 1963, the trend lines in Vietnam were clearly not favorable to the US Government nor its allies in Saigon. A dramatic response, or at least a re-thinking of strategy, was badly needed.

In response, a high-level US Government team met on November 21st in what was referred to as a Vietnam Summit. The chosen locale for the meeting was a Marine Corps base on the island of Oahu in Hawaii called Camp HM Smith. The base also housed secure facilities for the headquarters of the Commander in Chief for the US forces in the Pacific region.

As befitting the subject matter, the attendees, hosted by Secretary of Defense Robert McNamara, included such senior officials as Secretary of State Rusk, National Security Advisor Bundy, CIA Director McCone, Ambassador Lodge and other senior administration officials.

The product of the conference was a National Security Action Memorandum. The document was called *NSAM 273*. It was drafted by McGeorge Bundy for submission to President Kennedy.

The performance of the CIA in North Vietnam had been a subject of hushed insider discussion within the Beltway. The informed belief was that JFK concluded that the CIA efforts in the denied areas of North Vietnam were simply not effective. The thinking was that it was about time to turn the project over to Defense and the military, in hopes of achieving the desired results.

Classified at the Top Secret level, NSAM 273 proposed several key points for JFK's consideration:

- The central objective for the USG was to assist the Government of South Vietnam against the Communist conspiracy
- Senior members of the USG in defense of the policy should be united and energetic in support of the policy

- The Government of South Vietnam should be persuaded to focus its efforts on the critical situation in the region of the Mekong Delta
- The levels of USG military and economic assistance to South Vietnam should not fall below those levels provided to the Diem regime
- Actions against North Vietnam – especially those launched from the sea – should be geared to a new level of effectiveness
- Planning should be developed for military action within 50 kilometers of the Laotian border
- It was urgent that no opportunity be lost to exert favorable influence within the nation of Cambodia

All participants of the summit were well aware of the fact that in July of that year, a decision had been made that unconventional operations external to South Vietnam, currently run by the CIA, were to be absorbed by the Defense Department. These operations were to be in the guise of the Military Advisory Command Vietnam/Studies and Observations Group (MACV/SOG). That decision was known as OPLAN 34-Alpha, otherwise known as *Operation Switchback*. The effective date for the turnover was to be January 1, 1964.

During a break in the procedures, the former Saigon COS and current Director of the Far East Division, Bill Colby, met with John McCone, the Director of Central Intelligence. Colby took advantage of the time to bring the Director up to date on the history of Project Tiger and its failure to effectively penetrate the enemy in the North, despite intensive efforts. He harkened back to similar disappointments – and loss of life - in China and Eastern Europe operations.

Colby was said to have based his past hopes for a successful Vietnam campaign on a pair of issues: the CIA-sponsored pacification and counterinsurgency actions and the success of the two Ngo brothers – both of whom were murdered within the past three weeks.

As to the intent of OPLAN 34-Alpha, insertion of agents into the North to conduct espionage and sabotage, Colby's comments were simple and predictive. "It isn't working," Colby confided, "and it won't work any better with the military in charge."

Later in the day, Colby offered the same prognosis to SecDef McNamara. "It won't work," he repeated.

McNamara listened agreeably but, in the end, he chose not to accept the advice. The military would soon run the covert operations in the North.

FORTY-THREE - PLAIN OF REEDS

Hiep Hoa, South Vietnam
November 23, 1963

November continued to be a somber month for US interests in-country. The latest tragedy involved the fate of the US Army's Special Forces camp at Hiep Hoa, located near the contentious region known as the *Parrot's Beak*.

The so-called *Parrot's Beak* area of Cambodia bordered on South Vietnam. The area was more formally known as the Cambodian province of Svay Rieng. It posed a danger both to the US and allied forces as it served as a major staging area for both the Viet Cong guerrillas and the regulars of the North Vietnamese Army. It was also one of the logistical endpoints of the Ho Chi Minh Trail.

It was from there, under internationally protected circumstances, that the Communist troops were able to rest, reinforce, re-arm and prepare to launch fresh assaults.

A key portion of the American military strategy was the development of fortified camps in the border areas. Their role was to resist Communist incursions. This was done via the efforts of the US Army Special Forces troops - the Green Berets. The SF soldiers trained local inhabitants who were termed the CIDG - or the *Civilian Irregular Defense Groups*.

By June of 1963, the Green Berets had trained several thousand CIDG members in roughly 800 villages. Admittedly the training provided was fairly scant by American standards, ranging from two to six weeks of tactical schooling per member. It was recognized that the preparation of the indigenous CIDG personnel was far below that of the typical American soldier.

The primary objective of the paramilitary CIDG project was as political as it was militaristic. The aim was to expand the influence of the Saigon government as well as to reinforce control of the remote border areas.

The general mission of the CIDG was: (a) to serve as strike force members, (b) to man observation posts, (c) to perform reconnaissance duties and, (d) on occasion, to conduct joint operations with the South Vietnamese Army.

In close proximity to the isolated territory of the Parrot's Beak on the Vietnamese side was a stretch of land referred to as the Plain of Reeds. It was there that the Special Forces had established two CIDG camps. These were located at Tan Phu - commanded by SF Detachment A-23 - and at Hiep Hoa - commanded by SF Detachment A-21. Each was a fortified primitive encampment, surrounded by villagers and agricultural fields and encompassing a small airstrip.

In the case of Hiep Hoa, the encampment was a fortified area of 125 by 100 meters overlooking a narrow canal. It was located roughly forty-five miles northwest of Saigon.

Established in July of that year, Hiep Hoa maintained a garrison of slightly over two hundred troops. Within its fortifications were four .30 caliber machine guns - one positioned on each of the four corners of the camp. These were supplemented by two 81 mm mortars.

Morale among the SF troops at Hiep Hoa was not high. Less than a month earlier - on October 29th - three SF soldiers had been ambushed by the VC and captured after a day-long fight. They had been in the local area while patrolling with the CIDG along the canal.

One of the Americans - Lieutenant Nick Rowe - would eventually spend five years as a prisoner of war prior to his escape and rescue. Twenty-four years later, Rowe, then a lieutenant colonel, would be assassinated by terrorists while serving as a US military attaché in the Philippines.

That November evening was little different in Hiep Hoa from any of the others. The CIDG troops and members of the surrounding villages completed their usual functions and, secure with their accomplishments, drifted off to sleep.

Shortly after midnight, the landscape exploded with violence as some five hundred VC fighters launched an all-out surprise attack on the compound.

Well aware of the camp's layout and defenses, thanks to reports that had been provided by infiltrators and sympathizers, the VC quickly overwhelmed Hiep Hoa's strong points. Quickly killing the guards, the VC turned the .30 caliber machine guns on the shocked defenders as they tumbled out of their billets in search of fighting positions.

The American commander, a Green Beret lieutenant named Colby, called into his headquarters for immediate air support. His request resulted in a series of napalm drops and strafing runs flown in an attempt to beat back the attackers.

The air support was all to no avail, as the attackers pursued their favored tactic of closing in with and effectively hugging the proximity of the defenders.

Seeing what was to be the inevitability of the camp's collapse in the din of battle, Colby ordered his SF troopers to evacuate the camp and begin to individually escape and evade in the surrounding countryside.

Despite their best efforts, all of the Americans were eventually captured. And with that, Detachment A-21 passed into Communist hands.

Hiep Hoa thus became the first Special Forces camp to suffer the indignity of being over-run by Communist forces in the Vietnam war.

* * *

Hours later, at the NVOB in Saigon, Koval called for a hurried emergency meeting of his staff. There had been no explanation. As they assembled in the wee hours of the morning, reaching for cups of black coffee, the CIA staffers became aware of the fall of Hiep Hoa. Their murmured private discussions focused on what this development bode for their operations both North and South.

Settling into their chairs around the chipped and marred conference table, Jim Koval reluctantly broke even more grim news: President John F. Kennedy had just been assassinated in Dallas.

FORTY-FOUR - DE SILVA

December 1963
Washington, DC

The country was still reeling from the traumatic events of late November. The charismatic aristocrat, JFK, was gone. In his place was the charisma-free pedestrian figure of LBJ – Lyndon Baines Johnson of Texas.

The life of the American President had been taken by a former US Marine named Lee Harvey Oswald.

Essentially a nonentity prior to November 22nd, the former Marine had been trained by the Corps as an Aviation Electronics Operator. He was then assigned to the Naval Air Facility in Atsugi, Japan. As it happened, Atsugi was one of the bases from which the Agency's U-2 aircraft were launched, soaring high over the Soviet Union.

While on active duty, Oswald exhibited an interest in all things Russian. Via independent study, he acquired a limited ability with the Russian language. However, more troubling to some of his fellow Marines, however, were his occasional political comments, which they perceived to be of a distinctly pro-Soviet nature.

Following his discharge in 1959, Oswald essentially defected to the USSR. There, he formally requested Soviet citizenship. After a brief time in Moscow, he settled in Minsk, the capital of the Byelorussian Soviet Socialist Republic.

It was in Minsk that he eventually met and married a Russian-born woman named Marina Prusakova. Her uncle was a Colonel in Ministry of Internal Affairs, or MVD.

The Agency suspected that the KGB could not have been unaware of Oswald's past connections with the U-2 program, however tenuous. And if such were the case, they would have found it difficult to resist approaching him for whatever information he might be able to provide.

Evidently tiring of Soviet life, in 1962 Oswald returned to the United States with his new wife and established a home in Dallas. Subsequent photos would emerge showing him passing out leaflets for something called *The Fair Play for Cuba Committee*.

Oswald was arrested on the 22nd, but not before shooting and killing a Dallas police officer named JD Tibbets. Two days later, on the 24th, he was himself was shot and killed while being moved from the Dallas police headquarters to a more secure location. The assailant, Jack Ruby, was a strip-club owner who was thought to have murky relations with the Mob.

Issues of domestic angst aside, there was still a war going on in Vietnam, and it was proceeding apace.

One of the issues calling out for resolution was the matter of replacing the Saigon Station Chief. Richardson's recall for ostensible consultations at the beginning of October had, in fact, marked his termination from post. His deputy had been running the Station ever since.

The name of the preferred replacement was a man who was a friend and colleague of Richardson's. It was CIA and OSS veteran Peer de Silva. A West Pointer, de Silva served throughout World War II and the Cold War in both Europe and Asia. He was currently assigned as the Chief of Station in Hong Kong.

De Silva was directed to fly to Washington immediately. There, he met with President Johnson, who approved his selection. Orders were cut, sending him forthwith to Saigon.

FORTY-FIVE - 34-ALPHA

Saigon
January 1964

Based upon the July 1963 agreement, the Studies and Observations Group/MACV-SOG was to be officially activated, or *stood up*, on January 24th. This was to be the implementation of OPLAN 34-Alpha.

As the new year began, Jim Koval and his officers were no longer focused on sending agent teams into the North and dealing with their various needs and issues. Rather, they worked on the shutdown of their offices and arranging the transfer of the operations to the new kids in town.

NVOB, the North Vietnam Operational Base, also known as *The Indochina Aid and Development Foundation*, was coming to an administrative conclusion. Its termination had been signed, sealed and – with the arrival of Clyde Russell in Saigon – delivered.

Koval accepted this with a sense of relief; a relief heavily tinged with a sense of failure.

Colonel Clyde Russell was an American warrior with a well-established history. A World War II veteran, he had jumped into France on D-Day as part of the 505th Parachute Infantry Regiment. Later, during the Korean War, he participated in MacArthur's landing at the port of Inchon, a risky enterprise that culminated in the re-capture of Seoul from the North Korean forces. Later in the 1950s, Russell found his way into the ranks of an organization that was not all that well-received in the senior ranks of the Army – the Special Forces.

And now, the penultimate levels of both the White House and the Joint Chiefs of Staff had selected him to be the SOG commander. Russell's background, however, did not prepare him well for what was to come.

For starters, Russell believed that he would be assuming control of an existing network of seasoned agent and resistance teams that were operating in the North. In truth, he was inheriting a mere five teams of indigenous agents that NVOB had previously inserted. As history would later indicate, all five teams had been compromised by the Communist security forces.

Russell and SOG would be essentially starting from scratch on that front.

Nor did it help that he was being staffed with a number of young Special Forces captains. Russell was soon to learn that, while his subordinates were fully qualified in the traditional SF missions, such as unconventional warfare and counterinsurgency, none had any experience in the recruitment, development and running of agent networks in denied areas.

North Vietnam was certainly a denied area.

Colonel Russell was also greeted upon his arrival by an announcement of the current President, Big Minh, that he opposed the presence of US troops in the villages. Minh went further to opine that the Americans might have actually been more imperialistic than were the French.

Whatever the case, Big Minh himself was to be overthrown by the end of the month by yet another ARVN general named Nguyen Kanh.

It was not an auspicious beginning for SOG.

FORTY-SIX - EXODUS

Saigon, South Vietnam
February 17, 1964

There had been yet another coup, this one far less violent than the first. Big Minh had been ousted, but he was still very much alive. On January 30th, he had been overthrown by another ARVN general officer.

The current President of South Vietnam was General Nguyen Khanh. A former ARVN Chief of Staff, Khanh was a 1946 graduate of the French military academy at St. Cyr. He had also attended the US Army's Command and General Staff College at Fort Leavenworth, Kansas.

General, now President, Khanh had been one of the original plotters, along with Minh, in the November coup. Following Minh's assumption of power, however, rather than being rewarded with a significant benefice he had actually been blocked from joining the twelve-man ruling Military Revolutionary Council, or MRC. He was then transferred north to Da Nang, which placed him even further from the seat of power in the capital. The actions did not sit well with him.

At the urging of several fellow disaffected generals, Khanh flew back to Saigon on the 28th and, on the morning of the 30th led the action against Minh and the MRC. He succeeded in deposing the government without the need for gunfire.

The reaction of the US Embassy to the second coup in fourteen weeks was far from negative. Ambassador Lodge cabled Washington with the news, commenting that now: *"We have everything we need in Vietnam. The United States has provided military advice, training, equipment, economic and social help and political advice... We have the means to do it. We simply need to do it. This requires a tough and ruthless commander. Perhaps Khanh is it."*

Well, perhaps.

Jay Laird was sitting in the departures area of the Tan Son Nhut passenger terminal. It was essentially where it had all started for him. He glanced up from his two-week-old copy of *Time* magazine to survey his fellow passengers.

He was only one of a handful of civilians in the group. The majority were uniformed members of the US military. A goodly number of them were in varying stages of inebriation. Others showed the effects of all-night celebrations, having survived a year or more in the war zone.

Some of the troopers were docile. One or two sat perfectly still, staring out of the window in a near-catatonic state. And there were those who showed no more expression than if they had been waiting for the next bus to Altoona.

Yet all were on their best behavior, or at least attempting to appear so. This was one flight they did not want to miss.

Laird turned his attention back to his news magazine, but, in truth, he was unable to focus on the stories. His mind was elsewhere.

Paul Sarpi had left post earlier in the week. He was going back to the States for a bit of home leave, after which he was being reassigned to one of his old haunts in Germany. They had plans to meet up in DC for a few beers within the next several days.

Herb, he of the *Sacred Sword of the Patriots League* fame, had been moved over from the Station to SOG. He was now functioning as a deputy and advisor to Colonel Russell. The military was interested in the SSPL concept and showed every intent to expand upon it.

Likewise, John Tate had voluntarily been seconded to SOG. He would be filling a slot in what they called *Op 39*. It was the psychological warfare component of the new organization.

The boss, Jim Koval, was still in Saigon and still working. He was attending to the various administrative tasks of closing down NVOB. When that was accomplished to the satisfaction of both the COS and Headquarters, he too would be departing. With regard to his future, Koval was noncommittal, but he seemed to have lost the fire in the belly.

As for Laird, he was on orders back to Washington. After a bit of his own home leave, he would be spending a year or more there immersed in Spanish language studies. That would be followed by his assignment to a branch of the Latin American division in the Langley Headquarters. And then back out to the field once again.

The cycle continues.

And there was the matter of Tuyet. She had cut her ties with SEPES and was currently in Hong Kong. Laird had asked her to go there for her own safety. With the help of de Silva's contacts, they were able to find reasonable accommodations for her in the British colony for the foreseeable future.

Laird assured her this was a temporary arrangement, and that he would send for her in America as soon as it was both practicable and possible. Although Tuyet had her doubts that she would ever see him again, she reluctantly agreed to the proposal.

Laird hoped that he could follow through on his promises to her.

FORTY-SEVEN - TONKIN

The Gulf of Tonkin
August 2, 1964

Officially, they were designated as *DeSoto Patrols*. These were intelligence-gathering missions undertaken by US Navy ships. The DeSotos were ships specially outfitted to monitor land-based electronic signals of the adversary.

Such patrols had been conducted off the coasts of North Korea, China and the Soviet Union itself. In 1964 they were collecting emanations along the coast of the Democratic Republic of Vietnam, i.e., North Vietnam.

The standing orders for the DeSoto Patrol ships, which were then classified at the Top-Secret level, were fairly explicit. The ships were directed to "... *locate and identify all coastal radar transmitters, note all navigation aids along the DRV's coastline, and monitor the Vietnamese junk fleet for a possible connection to DRV/Viet Cong maritime supply and infiltration routes.*"

One of the DeSotos, the USS Maddox, took up its station on July 31st. Although the facts have been disputed, the reporting stated that on the afternoon of August 2nd, while twenty-eight miles offshore, it was attacked by three North Vietnamese torpedo boats of Soviet origin. Presumably, the attack was launched in response to MACV-SOG maritime raids that occurred the previous day.

Following the emergency call from the captain of the Maddox, four carrier-based F-8 Crusader aircraft swept in and strafed the torpedo boats, eliminating the threat.

The Maddox was later joined by another ship – a destroyer, the USS Turner Joy. No less an authority than President Lyndon Johnson ordered that the two ships were to continue with the DeSoto mission.

The weather was bad on the evening of August 4th. Both ships acting on radio, sonar and radar returns, opened fire on presumed radar targets. No visual sighting of any North Vietnamese targets, however, was reported.

On the 5th, President Johnson ordered air strikes on North Vietnamese naval and infrastructure targets. Scant days later, on August 10, Congress approved the Gulf of Tonkin Resolution, giving him the authority to use military force, absent a formal declaration of war.

Six months later, on March 8, 1965, 3,500 members of the 9th Marine Expeditionary Brigade came ashore in Danang, South Vietnam. It was the first large-scale commitment of US combat ground troops.

It would not be the last.

FORTY-EIGHT - MONUMENTO

Venice, Italy
October 30, 2005

A lone figure, seemingly mindless of the time, stood gazing at the sea-green, patinaed statue. To the local Venetians, the colorful *Americano* was something more than a traditional tourist. He was a familiar personage who interacted with them on a regular basis. Especially at this time of the year.

The seventy-four-year-old fellow was a slightly built man who walked with a bit of a limp. He wore glasses and sported a trimmed beard. Tufts of longish graying hair sprouted from under his tweedy flat cap. While hardly fluent in the language, he nevertheless spoke passable Italian and conveyed a sardonic sense of humor.

It was early on a Sunday afternoon in the lagoon. The weather had cooled, and the majority of the foreign travelers had since departed. As was often the case, after lingering over a cappuccino at a favored *café bar*, he paused along his strolls at the *Campo Santa Fosca*.

The campo rested on one of the hundred-plus islands, both natural and manmade, that comprised the venerable Commune of Venice. *La Serenissima* boasted twelve centuries of history. Or more. The old earthen villages enclosing the campos were joined to each other with a variety of stone and wooden walking bridges. Aside from boats, foot traffic was the only option. There were no motorized land vehicles in the city.

In keeping with his usual practice, he had stopped to pay homage to the monument of Fra Paolo Sarpi. As he had related to Jay Laird, back in the day, he was the namesake of this very Servite monk who ran seriously afoul of the papacy in the year 1607.

Family lore held him to be a distant relative of Paolo. The fact, as they say, was too good to be verified.

Fra Sarpi's crime was that he served as the theologian who defended Venice when Pope Paul V placed it under an interdict, essentially a communal excommunication. It was a measure designed to make the city-state a pariah in the eyes of all of Christianity, destroying its economy and much else.

Black Entry

Based upon his astute arguments, as well as the aggressive posture of the Commune in defending its interests, the papal effort failed. It was a disaster for the public image of the Church and its authority over Catholic Europe.

It was, therefore, on this spot – or very near to it – that the three papal assassins set upon Fra Sarpi. The attackers repeatedly stabbed him and left him for dead. But the monk, like his Twentieth Century descendent, survived the crisis. He lived another sixteen years, and survived two more attempts on his life, until his death in 1623.

Thanks to an inheritance from his fairly well-to-do family, Paul Sarpi spent a few months each year living in Italy. Not in Venice proper though – too expensive – but across the lagoon on the mainland. In Mestre.

The rest of the year, he spent at home in his condo in Northern Virginia.

For several of those months at home, Sarpi worked as a *Green Badger*, or a part-time contractor, at *the Building*, Agency Headquarters, in Langley to supplement his pension. He did it to stay busy and involved, at least to some degree.

Most recently, he had been assisting some of the Analysis people on the Iraqi account. Before that, he was assigned to work on a variety of Baltic issues.

He was willing to pitch in on anything. Anything, that was to say, except those matters related to Southeast Asian affairs. He wanted no part of the region since his departure from NVOB and Saigon Station.

Some dozen years after the closure of NVOB, on May 1, 1975, to be exact, Sarpi had been on a TDY trip to West Germany. Following visits to the CIA offices in Bonn and Frankfurt, he had taken a few days off for a bit of sightseeing. His travels initially took him to the twelfth-century Hessian town of Gelnhausen, situated midway between Frankfurt and the East German border.

The news broadcast that he watched in his hotel room that evening was disturbing but hardly unexpected. It focused on the culmination of a North Vietnamese offensive that had been launched weeks earlier. It was unexpected insofar as Agency analysts had grown increasingly pessimistic about the odds of success in Vietnam, especially during the years of 1964 and 1965.

One of the Station officers who had been on-site during the frantic closing hours of the evacuation later described the situation as, "... an absolute nightmare. Especially in the last twelve hours while we were in the Station. We were in the process of destroying not only the files but all of the commo gear as well... All along, in the background, we could hear the frantic voice communications coming in from the outside. The traffic was all sheer panic... I still try to erase it from my memory. But I can't."

The officer went on to quote the Chief of Station, just prior to the pull-out, observing that, "The goddamn thing is over, except for the crying."

On April 30th the North Vietnamese troops forced entry into the capital, even as the US helicopters of *Operation Frequent Wind* pulled the final evacuees out of Saigon.

The American helicopters were followed by ARVN choppers who flew their own people out to the unsuspecting US Navy ships. Unable to receive the aircraft, the civilian evacuees were taken aboard, and the helicopters were pushed over the side and into the depths of the South China Sea.

Surprisingly, there was no hostile action from the Communists interfering with the evacuation. "I think they just wanted us to leave," said a Station officer.

By the end of the day, the Communists had finally won the long and bitter struggle.

Sarpi propped a foot up on a bench and began to massage an aching knee. He had initially feared that knee surgery might have been looming in the future. But no. Arthritis, the doctor said. Could have been worse.

Straightening up, he caught sight of an attractive young Asian woman who was crossing the campo with several friends. Chattering and happy, she could have been a sister of the younger Tuyet.

Tuyet *Laird*, he mentally corrected himself. He had not seen her in decades. The last that he knew, she was still a widow, now twice over, living among the Vietnamese community – also somewhere in Northern Virginia.

Sarpi recalled that Tuyet had herself once been under suspicion of being a VC agent. The allegations were related to leaks coming from the SEPES office, endangering Project Tiger. For several months, she had been investigated by the Station's CI section. The case on her – never very solid to begin with - was eventually closed, having failed to uncover any substantive or derogatory information.

As to the fate of Jay Laird himself, that was a bit more complex.

Sarpi, although still affiliated with the CIA, was not cleared to know the details of the final days of his former colleague. Stories in the Agency, such as they were, circulated about his loss in the Central American country of El Salvador.

Whatever occurred happened circa 1986 or 1987.

Supposedly, Laird had been assigned as an intelligence advisor to the Salvadoran military headquarters, otherwise known as the *Estado Mayor*. As the tale unfolded, Laird had accompanied a Salvadoran Army unit on an operation in the province of La Union, close to the Honduran border in eastern El Salvador.

There was a clash between the government troops and the Communist FMLN guerrillas. That much was known.

The story blurred from that point. Laird never returned. Nor was a body ever recovered.

He knew that Laird did have an anonymous star on the CIA Memorial Wall at Headquarters. For what it was worth.

Sarpi's old friend and boss from both the Saigon and Berlin years, Jim Koval, had also passed on. Somewhat disgruntled, Koval left the Agency a few years after the close of NVOB. Former colleagues gradually lost touch with him. The consensus was that he appeared to have been seeking isolation from current events.

Word had it that he eventually died of a heart attack in his native Ohio.

And then there was John Tate, the last of Sarpi's NVOB cell mates. Apparently, a glutton for punishment, he spent another half year in Vietnam working with MACV-SOG after the closure of NVOB. But eventually, enough was enough. Even for a hardass like him.

Harkening back to his Special Forces days, Tate cut ties with the Government and moved to North Carolina. There he bought a house in the town of Southern Pines, not far from Fort Bragg. That was where he lived with his Cuban-American wife until he reached his early 'eighties, when time and toil finally caught up with him.

As an NVOB veteran, Sarpi had been privy to an after-action review of the Project Tiger operation. In sum, it had not been complimentary to their joint efforts.

According to the review, the Agency had failed in allowing their well-penetrated South Vietnamese allies to select the majority of the agents who were to be sent North, thus dooming them in retrospect. This was exacerbated by the lack of intelligence networks on the ground to receive them. They were blind-dropping most of them over uncoordinated areas, unlike the situation that existed in Nazi-occupied Europe in World War II.

Earlier in the year, Sarpi had seen a classified review of the NVOB operations published by the Agency's in-house think tank, *The Center for the Study of Intelligence.*

The article detailed the NVOB activities in North Vietnam and went on to speculate as to why the Agency continued to pursue the operations for some three years, later supporting similar projects conducted by MACV-SOG. All had resulted in heavy losses with negligible results.

Among other things, the author referred to a 1959 conference regarding the similar Eastern European operations in which Koval had been involved. A former Berlin Chief opined that the whole effort had then been a waste of time. Referring to the fate of the agents who were dropped into the Soviet-controlled areas of Eastern Europe, he concluded that, "We might just as well shoot them."

Answering his own question, the author noted that, by the Spring of 1961, the CIA was under considerable pressure, via Presidential order, to do something to counter the mounting Communist threat to South Vietnam.

The conclusion of the piece was sobering: "The question remains whether any Agency manager would ever have taken the same risks, for so little reward, if these operations had required even a token CIA presence. It is certainly true that the GVN tolerated its casualties, not all of whom were merely expendable members of despised minorities.

"This willingness, it seems, served to legitimize for CIA the exposure of dozens of Vietnamese agents to a degree of risk that no Agency manager would ever have contemplated imposing on his own people."

An earlier researcher had claimed that, of the more than five hundred long-term agents who were sent North by either the CIA or by MACV-SOG, none were successfully exfiltrated back to South Vietnam. Presumably, all were captured having then turned or executed. Comparisons were made with Britain's successful *Double Cross* network, which caught, turned, and then ran all of the German agents sent into the country during the Second World War.

So, there you have it.

Sarpi pulled off his cap and stood for a moment, twisting it between his hands. Blinking his eyes, he bowed his head and offered a silent prayer for the souls of his departed colleagues. And for all the members of the lost agent teams who gave their trust along with their lives. And for everyone involved in the whole damn enterprise.

Sarpi replaced his cap, tugged it down over his forehead, and looked up into the face of the statue.

"Amen."

-END-

Acknowledgements

For background and related information on Vietnam and CIA operations in and against North Vietnam and North Korea:

Ahern, Thomas - "The Way We Do Things: Black Entry Operations into North Vietnam, 1961-1964" Center for the Study of Intelligence (CIA), Washington, DC, 2005 (Declassified)

Briggs, Thomas Leo - "Cash on Delivery - CIA Special Operations During the Secret War in Laos" Rosebank Press, Rockville, MD, 2009

Budiansky, Stephen - "Code Warriors: NSA's Codebreakers and the Secret Intelligence War Against the Soviet Union" Vintage, 2016

Celeski, Joseph – "Special Air Warfare and the Secret War in Laos: Air Commandos 1964-1975" Air University Press, 2019

Chamberlin, Paul Thomas – "The Cold War's Killing Fields: Rethinking the Long Peace" Harper, New York, Ny, 2018

Conboy, Kenneth & Andrade, Dale - "Spies and Commandos: How America Lost the Secret War in North Vietnam" University of Kansas Press, Lawrence, KS, 2000

(Contributor) – "The Storied History of Caravelle Hotel in Ho Chi Minh City" Destin Asia, May 2, 2009

Dimitrakis, Panagiotis - "Secrets and Lies in Vietnam: Spies, Intelligence and Covert Operations in the Vietnam Wars" I.B. Tauris & Co., New York, NY, 2016

Friedman, Herbert (US Army, SGM Retired) - "The Sacred Sword of the Patriots League" www.psywarrior.com

Gralley, Craig (Editor) – "Voices From the Station: The Evacuation of the US Embassy in Saigon" Center for The Study of Intelligence (CIA), Washington, DC, April 2005 (Declassified)

Grant, Zalen – "War Stories" www.PythiaPress.com/wartales/spy

Jacobsen, Annie - "Surprise, Kill, Vanish: The Secret History of CIA Paramilitary Armies, Operators and Assassins" Little, Brown and Company, New York, NY, 2019

Hammond, William – "The US Army in Vietnam - Public Affairs: The Military and the Media, 1962-1968" Center for Military History, Washington, DC, 1990

Hancock, Larry & Wexler, Stuart - "Shadow Warfare: The History of America's Undeclared Wars" Counterpoint Press, Berkeley, CA, 2014

Kelly, Francis, "Vietnam Studies - US Army Special Forces 1961-1971" Department of the Army, Washington, DC 2004

Kwon, Heonik - "Ghosts of War in Vietnam" Cambridge University Press, Cambridge, UK, 2008

Kurlantzick, Joshua - "A Great Place to Have a War: America in Laos and the Birth of a Military CIA" Simon and Schuster Paperbacks, New York, NY 2016

Paterson, Pat – "The Truth About Tonkin" Naval History Magazine, February 2008, Vol. 22, No. 1, US Naval Institute, Annapolis, Maryland

Prados, John and Nichter, Luke (editors) – "New Light in a Dark Corner: Evidence on the Diem Coup in South Vietnam, November 1963", National Security Archive, November 1, 2020

Rottman, Gordon - "Special Forces Camps in Vietnam 1961-1970" Bloomsbury Publishing, NY 2011

Shultz, Richard H. – "The Secret War Against Hanoi: The Untold Story of Spies, Saboteurs, and Covert Warriors in North Vietnam" HarperCollins, NY, 2000

Toczek, David M. – "The Battle of Ap Bac, Vietnam" NavalInstitute Press, Annapolis, MD, 2007

Vo, Nghia M. – "Saigon: A History" McFarland and Company, Jefferson, NC, 2011

Woods, Randall B. – "Shadow Warrior: William Egan Colby and the CIA" Basic Books, NY 2013

www.historynet.com/a-study-in-terror.htm

www.thoughtco.com/vietnam-war-gulf-of-tonkin-incident-2361345

https://military.wikia.org/wiki/Battle_of_Ap_Bac

https://worldhistoryproject.org/1963/8/21/xa-loi-pagoda-raids

www.pbs.org/reportingamericaatwar/reporters/halberstam/coup.html

* * *

For background information on British and American operations in post-war Albania:

Lulushi, Albert - "Operation Valuable Fiend: The CIA's First Paramilitary Strike Against the Iron Curtain" Arcade Publishing, New York, NY 2014

* * *

For general information on CIA tradecraft:

Hoffman, David, "The Billion Dollar Spy: A True Story of Cold War Espionage and Betrayal" First Anchor Books Edition, New York, NY, 2015

Hood, William, "Mole: The True Story of the First Russian Intelligence Officer Recruited by the CIA" W.W. Norton & Co., Inc., New York, NY, 1982

Kempe, Frederick - "Berlin 1961: Kennedy, Khrushchev, and the Most Dangerous Place on Earth" Berkley Books, NY, 2011

* * *

For general information on Fra Paulo Sarpi of Venice:

Robertson, Alexander - "Fra Paulo Sarpi: The Greatest of the Venetians" Hardpress Publications, Miami, FL, 2014

CPSIA information can be obtained
at www.ICGtesting.com
Printed in the USA
BVHW071649300122
627515BV00001B/58

9 781506 907437